GIFTS
AND OTHER STORIES

GIFTS
AND OTHER STORIES

Charlotte Holmes

A James R. Hepworth Book

CONFLUENCE PRESS

ACKNOWLEDGMENTS

Grateful acknowledgment is made to the editors of the following magazines in which many of these stories first appeared.

The Antioch Review, "Guitar;" *Carolina Quarterly*, "Field;" *Epoch*, "Migrations;" *Grand Street*, "Buddy," "Metropolitan" (which also appeared in *New Stories from the South: The Best of 1988*); *The New Yorker*, "Thanksgiving;" *STORY*, "Gifts," "World Book."

My thanks, too, to the Pennsylvania Council on the Arts, to the writing program at Stanford University, and to Pennsylvania State University, for research grants that made completion of these stories possible.

And to my teachers: deepest gratitude.

First Edition

ISBN 1-881090-05-1 (paper) / 1-881090-04-3 (cloth)

LIBRARY OF CONGRESS CARD NUMBER 93-71410

Publication of this book is made possible by grants from the Idaho Commission on the Arts, a State agency, and the National Endowment for the Arts in Washington, D.C., a Federal agency.

Cover design: Karla Fromm
Production and text design by
Darinda Schmidt and Tanya Gonzales

Published by:

Confluence Press, Inc.
Lewis-Clark State College
500 8th Avenue
Lewiston, Idaho 83501

Distributed to the trade by:

National Book Network
4720-A Boston Way
Lanham, Maryland 20706

For James Brasfield
and for Stanhope

CONTENTS

Gifts make slaves, the Inuit say.
Just like whips make dogs.

World Book

BEHIND THE PINES screening the bus stop, the Georgia sun is so bright and small, it looks like a dime lost under a grating. Cora squints up, shutting one eye so she won't go blind. Then she looks at the street, dimmed now and narrowed. A woman raking leaves in the opposite yard blurs white against the yellow sweet gum trees. A pale shape advancing on the road wavers like a fish rising out of dark waves. Cora hops on one foot, feeling weighted by her wool coat and new red hat; she holds out her arms and whirls in a circle to see the jumbled world wheel past.

"Quit that," her mother says, plucking at her shoulder. "You'll make yourself sick."

Cora stops and the images fall into place like a deck of cards shuffled, then stacked on the table. She looks up at her mother, who seems to vibrate for a moment. Maxine wipes her nose with an embroidered handkerchief and stares back at Cora as if she can't quite place her. Cora watches, mouth open slightly, breathing hard as Maxine bends the long distance down and opens Cora's fist.

"There," Maxine says, closing Cora's fingers around the token. "You can drop it in when the bus comes."

The red and white Augusta Transit bus accelerates across the intersection. Cora and her mother line up in front of the woman in the maid's uniform who was waiting at the stop when they arrived. The doors of the bus flap open and Cora swings herself onto the steps.

She used to call any man in uniform "Daddy," but now she knows that a bus driver is not her father; when this one says, "Good morning, Red Riding Hood, you going to Grandma's today?" she says only that her grandmothers live with Jesus.

3

She drops the token into the token box, then pleads with Maxine to sit in the long bench seat at the back of the bus, the one facing forward so she can see all the passengers and the scenery moving past.

"I'm prone to motion sickness," Maxine says. "I wouldn't sit back there if President Eisenhower himself issued me a special invitation. Besides," she whispers, pushing Cora into an empty seat up front, "we're not darkies."

Cora turns and sits on her knees in the seat. The rear of the bus is empty except for the maid who got on with them.

"Sit down," Maxine says, and turns her around.

"I hate you," Cora says.

"I'll slap your face right here," Maxine says, holding up her palm. "Apologize."

"No," Cora says, turning her face to the window as the bus lurches back onto the road. She pulls her coat collar up around her cheeks and presses her forehead against the glass, but Maxine jerks her shoulder.

"Look at me."

Cora feels her mother's sharp fingers on her chin and turns her head a half turn, facing forward. Maxine's breath smells of coffee as she leans close. "Don't you ever talk to me like that again."

Cora looks sideways at the gold circle pin on Maxine's black collar; on the bottom rim are three birthstones in a row and the clear one stands for her. She puts her finger on the stone she likes best, the pretty purple one, though Sis argues that this first stone can never be Cora's, that Cora will always have the chip of clear glass after Russ's opal.

Maxine's hand clamps down over hers. "Do you hear me?"

"No," Cora says.

The street where the bus lets them off is red clay, and Cora, though she's only five, knows the houses on this street are not as nice as her house. Maxine holds her hand tightly as they walk past flat-roofed ranchers where the grass needs cutting and the front windows are smudged. In a few of the front yards, dogs bark and pull against their chains as Maxine and Cora walk past, but one unchained white spitz comes running, barking, toward them over the scrappy lawn. Cora screams and Maxine picks her up. The screen door of the house flies open and a man in his undershirt peers out at them.

"Buster," he shouts and the dog stands still, barking at them from the grass. The dog's gums are black and shiny above his yellow teeth. His body jerks back with each bark and he braces his feet wide to steady himself. Cora presses her face into Maxine's shoulder and her mother starts walking again, teetering in her high heels under Cora's weight.

"I have to put you down," Maxine says, and Cora kicks her legs and cries, "No, that dog'll bite me."

"He won't bite you, crybaby," Maxine says, and sets Cora down on the road. "We've passed him. Look. Mr. Pool's house is right here."

Mr. Pool's is the only house Cora has ever seen with pink shutters. They are baby pink, as pale as her nightgown, and that color against the red bricks makes her stomach feel strange. Maxine tugs her hand. "Come on, I'm already late."

They step around bikes in the yard, a tricycle, a plastic duck flipped over on its back in a puddle. A football's on the front step, and Maxine pushes it into the bushes with the toe of her patent leather pump. Cora presses her face against the dirty screen and stares at the deep scratches in the pink door.

"Stop that," Maxine says, and rings the bell.

"Who made those scratches?"

"How am I supposed to know?" Maxine says, patting her hair. She's done it up for the occasion in a French Twist, a name that always makes Cora think of something good to eat.

"Maybe they had a dog one time," Maxine says, looking at the scratches herself now, but Cora shakes her head. Cora's new hat is felt, with a false blond ponytail sewn to the back and red ribbons under her chin. Maxine says it makes her look like a German girl, like Heidi from the storybook. Cora can feel the ponytail swing back and forth behind her.

"Kids made those scratches," Cora says, and rakes her nails over the screen.

Mrs. Pool opens the door. She's taller than Maxine, and blond, with a line of dark roots around her forehead. "Well, Miz Drayton," she says. "Frank was wondering . . . I just this minute got off the phone to y'all's house." She pushes the screen door open with one hand and stands back to let Maxine and Cora in.

The Pools' house smells of cigarettes and bacon. Cora presses herself against Maxine's legs and turns her face against her mother's black coat. In the living room the adults sit around in folding chairs, legs crossed, clipboards across their knees. "Hey, Maxine!" a woman says, and Maxine answers brightly, "I thought I'd never get here!" Then, lowering her voice, "That damned bus was late again," as though Cora can't hear.

"Miz Drayton, here's a chair," Mr. Pool says, annoyed, and Cora feels her mother being guided away from her.

Mrs. Pool's hand comes down around Cora's shoulder. "The kids're downstairs in the rec room," Mrs. Pool says. "Come on with me and leave your mama alone."

Cora lets Mrs. Pool pull her a few feet away before she stops and begins to cry.

"Now, precious, what's wrong?" Mrs. Pool says in a high sing-song, still pulling her toward the basement stairs.

"I want to stay with Mama," Cora says. She holds on to the back of the nearest chair, where a young man with a crewcut turns and frowns at her politely, his head tilted to the side. Like the other men in the room, he wears a white shirt, black tie and black pants. His black shoes shine. Cora stares at them, still sniffling, then at her mother's patent leather shoes. "Mama?" she says.

"Now Cora," Maxine says from across the room. She's slipping her coat off, folding it over the chairback.

"Come on, sugar," Mrs. Pool says, pulling at Cora's arm. "The kids'll be glad to see you again."

Cora's fingers tighten around the gray metal chair. "No," she says. "Don't touch me."

"Well, let's get this show on the road, folks," Mr. Pool says, looking down at Cora. Standing in the center of the circle of chairs, he's already tired, with deep folds on either side of his small hazel eyes. His brown hair glistens under the overhead light, and as he opens his blue binder, he bends his head like a preacher ready for the choir to stop singing the offertory hymn. "Miz Drayton, you want to take your little girl downstairs so we can get started?"

"I'm not going downstairs. Those kids are mean," Cora says, and the adults, except Maxine and the Pools, laugh.

"Cora," Maxine says in a cheerful voice. "Come over here."

Maxine gives Cora two bank deposit slips and a pencil from her pocketbook and whispers, "You better not make a sound or I'll spank you right here, in front of everybody."

Cora sits in the dusty corner behind her mother's chair and pretends she is a secretary. She takes off her coat and straightens her Heidi hat, crosses her legs and props the slips of paper on her thigh. Pencil poised, she intends to write down everything they say.

"Ladies and gentlemen," Mr. Pool says, addressing his congregation of five people with varying degrees of desperation in their eyes. They look at him obediently; the two women even smile. Mr. Pool lifts his hands like Noah testing for rain, and says, "Welcome back. We're ready to begin the second day of sales training for *World Book Encyclopedia.*"

Cora stares at the black seams up the back of her mother's legs. For the past two days she's dressed up in her Sunday clothes after Cora's father has gone to work and Sis and Russell have gone to school, and taken the bus across town to the Pools'. Cora puts the tip of the pencil on the front of the deposit slip and traces down the short black line that separates dollars from cents. "One. Two. Three," she counts the lines the pencil passes over. She feels Maxine look at her and then away, and pushes herself deeper into the corner. Mrs. Pool's house is dirtier than their house; the corner's dusted with crisp flies and gray puffs that look like cat's fur, though Cora hasn't seen a cat. The Pools have beige wall-to-wall carpeting, and Maxine said yesterday she wanted that instead of her hardwood floors, too difficult to care for. In the corner behind Maxine's chair, a heating grate crimps the carpet. Cora puts her ear to it, listening for the kids, but all she hears is Mrs. Pool singing "Jingle Bell Rock" in the laundry room.

The kids are Tina and Cooter and Nancy, and nobody's old enough for school except Cooter, who's eight and home this week with a virus. Cora isn't sure how many of them belong to the Pools. They'd already formed a gang by the time she agreed to go down there yesterday. Even Nancy, who's only four, sat on her chest and drooled spit in her face while the other two punched and tickled her.

Maxine has on the same navy blue suit she wore yesterday, with a different blouse. Cora reaches up and pats her mother's bottom through the opening at the back of the folding chair. The wool tickles Cora's palm and she moves her hand from side to side, feeling for the flap of the zipper.

"Stop that," Maxine whispers, bending down.

Maxine's mouth is red, waxy as the apples in the bowl at home. Cora bows her head and puts her pencil against the paper. Apple-core was what the kids called her yesterday. Then, Apple-head. She draws a circle under the line she's traced on the deposit slip, and makes dots for eyes, nose, a downturned crescent for a mouth. The pencil point punches through the paper, against the knee of her corduroy pants. She lets it move onto the narrow wale of the fabric, a car tearing out, traveling down a highway, trailing a line of gray smoke the way their yellow car did before her father sold it. She had loved that car, but it was always breaking down. Now her father drives a dark green Olds that runs, he says, like a top. But it frightens her. When her father's home, it squats like a muddy frog in the driveway.

She pulls the pencil up to her belly and onto the stripes of her thin knit shirt, and makes a square on the yellow stripe where their house is. Next door, on the red, would be the Zimmermans' house but on the other side is an undeveloped lot, a little square of leftover woods where nobody lives. She draws a tree on the green stripe and drives past.

In the center of the room, Mr. Pool holds up a map and guides his finger down a curved line. "Right here is where I want to start," he says. "Sand Hills."

Mr. Pool looks from face to face, gauging the impact of his words. Maxine straightens the collar of her blouse, sits a little taller. "Now, I know yer thinking, 'how in the world can somebody like me sell encyclopedias to a lady in a fine house up there in Sand Hills.'" Mr. Pool nods, waiting. "But I tell you, nothing is impossible if you just have confidence in yerself. When you ring that doorbell, don't say, 'maybe I'll sell this book.'" He taps his finger at the place on the map. "You say, 'By God, I am going to sell this book.' I want everbody to learn that. I want everbody to believe that, too. And you'll see it's true. Word into deed. I want everbody to remember that when you start ringing doorbells in Sand Hills this morning."

Maxine's high heels snag the carpet as she jiggles her legs. "How long will we be out, Mr. Pool?" she wants to know.

He eyes her warily. "Why?" he says.

She clears her throat. "Well, it's just . . . I wasn't expecting to be away from home a long time today."

"Miz Drayton," Mr. Pool says, drawing the name out. Maxine's heels stop moving. Cora's stomach tightens, the way it does in Sunday school when she spills paint on the floor and the teacher smiles and says, Next time our Clumsy Cora will be more careful, won't she? and the other kids laugh.

"Miz Drayton." Mr. Pool lays the map down on his chair and puts his hands together into a temple. Cora watches him and thinks, Here's the church, here's the steeple, open the door and see the people. And inside her head she hears Sis shrilling "Which one's you?" because she's always fooled when she picks out a finger, always hurt when Sis says, "I forgot to tell you, it's a nigger church."

Mr. Pool gazes at his fingers pressed together, then looks up. "One thing you better learn, Miz Drayton," he says. "And this goes for all of you." He looks at them in turn, severely now, as if he can see to the bottom of their shiftless hearts. He even looks at Cora peering from behind her mother's chair, as if she has something to do with Maxine's reluctance to sell. "If you want to work for me, you've got to be prepared to work hard. Nobody in this world ever got to the top without putting in some mighty long hours."

Maxine starts to speak but he silences her, holding up his hand. "Sure, you got other things to do. But at *World Book* we want you to remember just one thing." He slips a heavy, hardbound book from under the map on his chair, and holds it before him like a shield. "Nothing in the world's more important than this book."

In pointed gold letters on the maroon binding is *Volume 1: Aardvark to Aztec*. With her pencil, Cora makes a capital *A* on the red stripe of her shirt, next to her house. A tiny hole appears in the thin cotton knit. She pulls, and the hole becomes a run, a road opening north and south.

The blue Rambler station wagon bumps out of the driveway and Cora turns from the smudged front window, crying, to face the children. They have surfaced from the basement playroom to gather stone-faced and silent behind Mrs. Pool. Nancy sucks the hem of her dress, raised to show her bare crotch; Cora knows that somewhere in the basement she'll find Nancy's wet pants, a wad of rank grayish nylon on the brown linoleum, and she cries louder, remembering the smell. Cooter jams his fists against his hips and frowns. "Whass wrong with that dope?" he says. "Why'd she have to come back?"

"Shut up," Mrs. Pool hollers, covering her ears. She swoops down, takes Cora by the shoulders and shakes her hard. "You little shit. Now stop that crying. Your mama'll be back sooner or later. You don't see none of the other kids carrying on like this, do you?"

"Yeah, you dumb crybaby," Cooter says. He wrinkles his

face and sticks it into Cora's. "Crybaby, crybaby, suck your thumb, wash it off with bubblegum."

"And you shut up, too, Cooter," Mrs. Pool says. "You damned kids get downstairs and take Cora with you. Let her play, now. I don't want no fussing." She runs a hand through her wavy yellow hair and glares at them. "The first one of you that sticks their snotty little nose up those stairs is going to catch the back of my hand."

"Yeah," Cooter says. "My mom means it, too." He wags his butt at her and heads for the stairs. Mrs. Pool calls him back to take Cora's hand, then pops him on the ear with her open hand when he comes close.

"Come on, crybaby," he says, tugging Cora by the arm, pulling her downstairs so fast she's afraid she'll fall.

In the basement nothing has changed. Though it's morning, the overhead light burns brightly behind the bug-speckled shade. Within the pale, glossy green walls, the only furniture is a brown plastic couch scarred with black electrical tape and a console TV with tape over all the controls; it's permanently tuned to a murmur on one station.

Tina, Cooter and Nancy rush the couch, pack themselves shoulder-to-shoulder across the cushions. Cora stands at the bottom of the stairs, sniffling.

"Hey Cora," Tina says in a sweet voice. "Would you like to watch TV with us?"

Cooter elbows Nancy. "Apple-core," he whispers.

Cora bows her head and the ribbons on her cap dig into her chin. Though Maxine told her to take the hat off, she likes the weight of the blond ponytail and the hair tickling against her neck. When she thinks of the hat, she's not Cora, but some other little girl, pretty and blond, from Woodlark or Xeno, Yinyin or Zoon, far-away lands she imagines waiting between the exotic letters at the end of the alphabet.

"Cora?" Tina says. "I said, do you want to watch TV?"

"What's on?" Cora says.

Cooter laughs. "She wants to know what's on," he says, and leans across Nancy to tickle Tina, but Tina ignores him.

"What's your favorite show?" Tina asks.

Cora thinks for a minute. "*Adventures in Paradise*," she says. Tina makes an astonished face. "*Adventures in Paradise!* Gosh, that's what's on right now."

Cora leans forward from the stairs, craning to see the television screen, and Nancy leaps off the couch and against her chest, knocking her to the floor. In an instant, the others are on her.

How long they hold her down on the brown linoleum and tickle under her arms, Cora doesn't know. Cooter and Tina let Nancy, being the smallest, do most of the work. She slaps Cora's cheek mechanically, with quick, popping sounds, and a wary, thrilled look's on her face as if she can't believe her own luck in being allowed to do this. Cora starts to cry out, but Cooter bends over her.

"Remember what my mom said," he whispers. "She'll wear your ass out if you bother her."

"Crybaby," Tina says, pinching her wrist. "You want to tell her how little old Nancy whupped your butt?"

"Apple-core," Cooter taunts. "Apple-head."

Tina grins, stroking the top of Cora's red felt cap. "Even her hat looks like an apple. She knows she's an apple-head."

"Don't touch my hat," Cora says.

"Y'all," Nancy says, rocking back onto Cora's stomach. "I'm tired of this. I wanna go outside."

"Cora'll tell," Tina says.

"We can fix that," says Cooter.

In the closet, the dark is black and heavy as her mother's wool coat, but scented with naptha, faded cologne, the spent, aching smell of feet. Cora knows by touch that she sits between a pair of work boots and a doll's house with the roof bashed in. Only a strip of light shines under the door Cooter locked before he and the others went outside to play. Cora listened to their feet bang up the stairs, listened for Mrs. Pool to ask what they had done with Cora, but all Mrs. Pool said was shut up so she could hear her stories on TV. Cora starts to call out, but hears tapping on the basement window and the children, muffled, laughing, "Apple-head, Apple-head, you still in there?"

In the back of the closet no one will tug at her clothes or slap her cheek. Cora feels the raw stitching where the ponytail used to be. She's afraid what her mother will say about the cap, bought at Woolworth's yesterday on the way home.

It is hours since her mother left her—hours, or even days or weeks since she woke this morning huddled in Sis's bed, then slid from the bed onto the cold floor, opened the door and stepped out into the hall. She heard her parents arguing in the kitchen, heard her mother say, "I wasn't born yesterday, Mister" and the oven door slam shut.

She stood at the kitchen door and watched her father drink down his coffee. It was early but he was already in his uniform, his cap and his briefcase on the table. He looked so angry, tall in stiff green wool, his brass and black shoes shining, that Cora wet her pants. "What are you doing up so early, Corey-gal?" he said, setting the coffee cup down on the table and swinging her up into his arms. "Pissy pants," he said to Maxine, standing teary-eyed beside the sink, "that's your department." He handed Cora over, picked up his briefcase and cap, and went quietly out the back door. Cora and her mother stood listening as her father started the Olds, as gravel spun into the street that led to the Army base. Then Maxine's hands were quick, snatching the wet gown off and slapping Cora's bottom. In the bathroom, her mother didn't make her take a bath, didn't seem to know what to do, why they were even there. Cora climbed into the tub and waited, but Maxine just stood with her hands over her face, her shoulders jerking, until Russ stumbled in in his underwear. He blinked when he saw their mother and then looked down at Cora in the empty tub. "You guys finished in here or what?" he said.

Cora knows she's in this closet until her mother comes back, or for as long as the other children mean for her to be. She's surrounded, as if the darkness is as penetrable as her imagination. Nights when she wakes in the room she shares with Sis, she drags blankets and pillows to the closet floor, where she makes a cocoon for herself, and dreams her sailboat, her teepee, her cabin in the wilderness. She tries to imagine how large the Pools' closet might be, and reaches out over the doll's house until she feels what at first seems to be the closet wall, but when she pushes, it gives a little under the pressure. "Boxes," she says out loud. Her voice sounds clear and matter-of-fact, surprising her in the darkness. She's in the hold of a ship, a stowaway among the cargo. She's in the attic of her grandmother's house where there was so much to throw away. She's under Sis's bed, surrounded by boxes of Girl Scout cookies that can't be sold because she's nibbled every one.

She climbs up on the stack of boxes and waves her hand until she finds and pulls the light cord. When the bare bulb comes on, she sees the boots, the broken toys, the rack of coats. Mostly, she sees plain brown boxes, all but one sealed with wide brown tape.

Cora pulls the flaps of the unsealed box open and looks inside. A few books are still there. She rubs her hand over the pebbly red cover of the volume on top, draws her finger over the simple, familiar shapes of the gold letters. She can't read many words yet, but can say the alphabet fast without a mistake, doesn't even trip anymore over the "L-M-N-O-P."

"B," she says, and traces it with her finger. She turns the pages slowly at first, looking at small gray photographs: a baboon, bacteria, a ballet dancer, a Bassett hound. She skims past the bayonnet, the bear, the diagram of cuts of beef, the bee burrowing into a rose, the bell, and past the birds, the boat, the brain, until she sees the bus. Here she stops. She puts her face close against the page to see inside the tiny windows, hoping to find her favorite seat, but daylight shines too brightly through every window. She feels in her pocket for the pencil Maxine gave her, then remembers that Cooter broke it. She would have drawn herself in, a tiny, smiling circle inside the square of light.

She turns the page, uncovering butterflies. In the black and white photographs they have the dull, banded bodies of the moths she sometimes finds on the curtains in the morning; when she plucks them off, they leave a residue as silky as Maxine's pink face powder on her hands. Cora traces her finger over the veined wings, the eyespots, the ugly bug-like bodies and slender antennae. In the gray close-up of wing scales, Cora sees fish scales instead, muted and faintly pearlescent. "Not the same," she says, putting her finger over the scales. "Which one's different?" Maxine will ask her at the grocery store, pointing to an orange someone left among the lemons, or "which one's different?" when she hangs socks on the clothesline; "which one's different?" when they set the table for supper because Cora still uses a smaller fork.

Cora closes the book. After a minute, she leans over and sticks her finger through an upstairs window of the battered doll's house.

"Here I am," she says, waving her finger around in an empty room.

Hours later, she wakes to her mother's voice, and Mrs. Pool's outside the door. Cora's neck is sore and her legs have gone to sleep.

"Mama?" she yells, when the door is unlocked. Mrs. Pool stands back and Maxine is there in her black coat, her black patent shoes.

Mrs. Pool exclaims, almost scolding, "There you are, you silly old gal! I thought we never would find you! Shame on you, hiding from us that way." And then, "God almighty, she's unpacked all those books! She can't open those!" Mrs. Pool snatches the book from the floor. "You better not have drawed in this," she says, examining it.

The red ribbons of Cora's cap cut into the soft skin under her chin and before anyone moves to touch her she begins to cry. The children are there in a row, and Mr. Pool, too, and as Cora stumbles out behind her mother, she looks at none of them, even as they follow her up the stairs. Her legs feel as if they're filled with bees. At the front door, she ventures

15

another look at her mother's face and sees it tight, shiny, a furious blushed mask that terrifies her in its strangeness.

"Mr. Pool," Maxine says, looking at no one. "I don't think we'll be back. I'm sorry if I've wasted your time."

Mr. Pool holds the screen door open and stands back to let them pass. ". . . just a damn nuisance," he mutters, looking down at Cora and then at the front steps strewn with toys. As Cora and Maxine pick their way across the littered yard, he calls out, "Anytime you change your mind, Miz Drayton, you've got my card."

When they step out into the road, Maxine says, "You didn't draw in that book, I hope. And what on earth happened to your hat? What were you doing in that closet in the first place?"

Maxine is holding Cora's hand tightly and Cora pulls it away. "I can hold my own hand," she says, showing her mother, but Maxine doesn't look. She sidesteps a puddle that Cora splashes through, then clicks her tongue. "Good Lord, Cora. Will you answer me? And watch where you're going. I hope we don't have to wait long for that bus."

Cora holds her hands out before her stiffly. She has her eyes fixed on her linked fingers and doesn't see the white spitz bounding across the rutted lawn. It doesn't bark until it's already begun to spring onto Cora's back, and knocks her face-down into the clay.

She's too scared to move. She hears the dog growling, feels its teeth tearing into her cap, into the thick fabric of her coat. She hears her mother crying for help, and finally a man yelling, "Buster, Buster," as he pulls the dog away. She turns her head and sees the man snap a leash onto the dog's collar. He kicks the dog hard in the ribs, kicks it all the way back a-cross the lawn and into the house, and closes the door behind them.

On the bus Cora sits beside her mother, who has been crying quietly since Cora said she was all right, that the dog didn't bite her, didn't even break her skin.

16

"But he could have killed you!" Maxine says, her voice rising plaintively as she pats the chewed lump of red felt that Cora holds in her lap. "Why people keep dogs like that, I'll never know. I'm just glad your daddy's not here. That old man'd be sorry he ever thought about having such a mean dog."

Cora pats her mother's hand, which looks startlingly white against the red felt, and her mother smiles at her but doesn't stop crying. They're on the downtown bus, crowded with midday shoppers. They're sitting on the sidewalk side and Cora is by the window, so she turns and looks out, still holding her mother's hand. The bus stops in front of Woolworth's and Cora thinks she could probably ask Maxine to buy her a pinwheel after all that has happened but she doesn't want to get off the bus, doesn't want to move.

Maxine puts her palm on Cora's forehead. "Are you tired, honey? You look a little tired. Maybe we'll both take a nap when we get home."

"No," Cora says. She gets up on her knees in the seat and puts her hands on either side of her mother's face. "Are you homesick?" she demands, thinking homesick is like carsick, seasick, airsick, words she knows because Maxine has been all of them.

Maxine smiles at her strangely. "Of course not, sugar," she says. "We've only been gone a few hours."

Cora's face is inches from her mother's, so close she can smell Maxine's cologne. "Well then, is Daddy?" she says.

Maxine laughs. She puts her hands over Cora's hands and draws them away from her face. "Homesick," she repeats, chafing Cora's fingers between hers. Cora looks steadily into the black centers of her mother's blue eyes. "No, honey," Maxine says. "I don't think he is."

"I'm homesick," Cora says.

"You are?" Maxine trills, looking down at herself and dropping Cora's hands. She hums "My Own True Love" in a trembling soprano and brushes at a few blond hairs stuck to her coat sleeve.

"Those kids hurt me," Cora says. "They tore up my hat."

Maxine stops humming. "Oh well," she says, and pats Cora's shoulder. "You've got other hats. And tomorrow we can stay home." She pushes the fine brown curls away from Cora's face and smiles. "Because," she says, "tomorrow is another day."

Out the bus windows, the downtown has already given way to the ordered, quiet streets of their neighborhood. Cora rubs her finger around and around the circle pin on Maxine's collar, bumping over the birthstones as if they were glass pebbles on the road.

Metropolitan

MR. HEBERT PARKED his green Impala in the lot beside the railroad tracks. I watched as he stepped from the car and locked the door. He smoothed back his hair with both hands like a swimmer surfacing, and glided across the street toward the Metropolitan. He moved slowly, in a limp black suit, yellowed shirt, and dark wool tie even in the hot Louisiana summer. His long face was criss-crossed with tiny red veins, and his skin hung loose, almost billowing from the cheekbones. He turned his head cautiously from side to side as he walked, as if he expected at any minute to be confronted. But no one stopped him. I saw him nod to an old man as they passed on the sidewalk, then quickly look away, toward the display window where the pink neon sign flashed "Metropolitan" off and on above dust-covered aspirin bottles, after shave lotions, and two heart-shaped boxes of white, rock-hard nougats and stale caramels. By the time the bell over the front door jingled, I was busy spraying Windex on the bevelled glass of the perfume counter.

"Good morning, Neva," he said. Mr. Hebert's voice was dry and cool.

I moved my dustcloth back and forth across the glass as I smiled and told him good morning. Mr. Hebert and I had exchanged few words since he'd hired me; in fact, he rarely spoke to anyone except Skelly. He was in the store a few hours each morning, and again before closing. The rest of the day, he worked as a land surveyor. Val-Jean told me that he wasn't interested in pharmaceuticals—that only a provision in his father's will kept him from selling the store. He'd closed down the soda fountain rather than keep it clean enough to be relicensed, and the polished oak counter had been rebuilt to house cosmetics. Perfume bottles and a few pieces of bright, cheap jewelry were scattered on the glass shelves of the pie case.

This morning Mr. Hebert did not walk past me as usual, but stood quietly at the counter. His eyelids were wrinkled and thick, and he blinked a little as he looked at the perfume displays.

"Neva," he said finally. "What have you done with my Wind Song?"

His question so startled me that I could feel my face growing hot, and I fumbled with my cloth.

"Over there, sir," I said, pointing to a cluster of crown-shaped bottles I'd arranged in a pyramid on the top shelf.

He looked at me severely, and then looked at the bottles. He looked back at me.

"Elegant," he said, and walked away.

I was temporary. I'd been working at the Metropolitan Drug Store for three weeks that summer. Val-Jean got me the job.

"We need a little high school girl to work part-time," she told my mother. "Somebody to help out over the summer so I can take some time off now and then."

She and my mother were talking on our back porch about tomato plants. She brought my mother a seedling in a plastic pot tied with an orange ribbon.

"Welcome to the neighborhood," I heard her call. "Sure hope you like termayters."

We'd moved to Beauville only a few days earlier. I was fourteen, and high school was still a year away, but I was pleased that Val-Jean had thought I was older. She lived with her husband in the house behind us. I'd seen her a few times barbecuing hamburgers in their backyard, but I'd never spoken to her. In the evenings when I helped my father clear the tangle of undergrowth from the shrubbery, I saw Val-Jean walking back and forth on the deck of her house in tight white shorts and a halter top. When she leaned over the grill, the vertebrae bulged along her spine. She looked twenty-seven or -eight, but her skin was already leathery with sun, and above the waistband of her shorts, a small ruffle of brown skin hung like the fluting on a pie crust. Her eyes were so brown they seemed pupiless, and I had never seen hair as coarse and dark as Val-Jean's.

"The color of a crow's wing," my father said once, when he stood to light a cigarette and caught me watching her.

It was past one, and Val-Jean was taking another of her long lunch breaks. All week she'd been taking off for two or three hours in the middle of the day. I got nervous if Mr. Hebert wandered into the store while she was gone, but he never asked where she was, or even seemed to notice that she was missing.

As I Windexed the glass, I heard him talking to Skelly at the back of the store. Skelly had a television set in the room where he filled prescriptions; he had a hot plate and a recliner. Green and amber bottles lined the shelves of his small chamber, and someone long ago had sewn print curtains for the two doors—one leading to the store proper, the other opening onto the supply room. Skelly's room was a gathering place for his friends and the salesmen from the drug companies. In the afternoons, they watched their stories on TV and drank the thick chicory coffee Skelly brewed. The only bathroom in the store was a cubicle at one side of the supply room, and when Skelly's friends were visiting, I didn't go back there. The men snickered when they heard the toilet flush, and when I came back through the door, they grinned. Skelly never interfered with them. He counted pills into bottles with his head bent and a thin smile on his face.

That afternoon I heard the shrill voices of cartoon characters from Skelly's TV as I wiped the caked lipstick from the samples on the Yardley display. I'd read that the model whose face sulked on the cardboard backdrop was friends with the Rolling Stones and didn't mind being six feet tall. I'd grown two inches taller that summer, and as I looked at my big hands fumbling among the lipsticks, I hated the knuckles, the wide, flat nails too broad for polish, the small brown freckle that had appeared at the base of my thumb the previous weekend. The lipsticks were pale beige, pink, apricot—colors iridescent as shell, almost glowing inside their clear cases. I put down my dustcloth and slipped the palest of the samples from the display.

"We had five hatch this morning," Skelly said as I leaned toward the mirror, and Mr. Hebert answered, "Five. Well, well. Five is a good number."

They were talking about Mr. Hebert's quail. Val-Jean said to me once that Mr. Hebert was interested in only two things, and the other one was his quail. I thought about this as I watched my lips turn pale and slick. The main thing Mr. Hebert was interested in was his surveying business, I supposed, but I was skeptical that the quail had competition. Mr. Hebert's visits to the Metropolitan seemed motivated by the nervous desire to see if they were hatching. The eggs incubated in the heat of the supply room. Boxes of laxatives, shampoos, and toothpastes had been pushed aside to make room for the wire and plywood frame that held the nests, and the effect was that of a shrine. Low-watt bulbs circled the frame and shone dully through the old bedspread that covered it. The smell in the room was overwhelming—a heavy, wild animal odor mixed with a wave of hot dust and the thin, sweet smell of the merchandise. I complained, but Skelly and Val-Jean said they couldn't smell anything.

They both warned me not to breathe a word about the birds to anyone—not even to my parents. I promised, though it seemed silly to think of so much secrecy over a few wobbling downies and the small white eggs there seemed to be more of every time I peeked into the supply room. Sometimes when I was waiting on customers out front, I heard the downies chip-chipping in the back room. I was always surprised that no one ever asked where the noise was coming from.

As I stepped back from the mirror, I thought that any other drugstore would be an oasis: cool, immaculate, the air drenched with the medicinal balm of healing. The clammy air that hung in the Metropolitan that afternoon left condensation on the display windows and smelled of wildlife and mildew. I opened my eyes until they were wide and startled looking, and pushed my tongue behind my bottom lip to create a pout that almost matched that of the Yardley girl. I tried to imagine how I might look to someone seeing me for the first time—how Mick Jagger might see me if he walked into the Metropolitan at that instant.

The bell over the front door gave a sharp, excited little ring as Val-Jean, returning from lunch, pushed open the door with one hand square on the glass. The faint, greasy print of her palm was the first thing I saw when I looked up from the mirror. She gave her chewing gum an emphatic pop and walked past me with her head bent as if looking at me would have been too much trouble. She put her purse into a drawer behind the counter and began poking in her hair with a comb.

"Bring me that Bubbling Burgundy sample, why don'tcha?" she said, keeping her back to me. She pointed with her comb to a lavish new display in which all the lipsticks were named after wine.

I picked out the tube of violent magenta high-frost. "But it's so dark, Val-Jean," I said.

She sniffed. "You think I'd look better wearing one of those shades like you've got on?" She pointed to the London Lights display. "One of those colors that makes you look like you've rubbed Clorox on your lips?"

"It's the style," I said.

"So what? I've got strong coloring," she said. "I can handle rich shades."

I handed her the lipstick. When she turned to take it from me, I saw the dark swelling that was beginning to settle beneath her left eye.

"Who hit you?" I said in wonder, reaching out to touch her face. I'd never seen a black eye in person.

She pushed my hand away. "I wish you could have seen how you looked when I walked in just now," she said. "Everybody walking past on the sidewalk probably saw you, too. You looked like you thought you were Miss America. You were so funny looking, I thought I'd die."

By two-thirty I was bored with polishing the glass. It was a terrible day. We had only two customers all afternoon. Val-Jean had been grumbling to herself behind the counter since her return, refusing to speak to me or wait on customers, refusing to do anything. Skelly and Mr. Hebert were still cloistered in the back room.

"Gotta be careful when they're this young," I heard Skelly say when I went to the back to ring up a sale, and Mr. Hebert answered, "Yessir. That's a true fact."

I gave up trying to look busy. Mr. Hebert had come from the back room only once since he entered it that morning, and that was to call for Val-Jean.

"Would you come here please, Val-Jean?"

She didn't budge. She looked out the window and picked at her fingernails. After a while, Mr. Hebert turned and went back into the room.

In the days when Mr. Hebert's father owned the store, the Metropolitan had been something of a hang-out. The soda fountain churned out frappes and sundaes to the beat of a Wurlitzer jukebox. The old Wurlitzer was still wedged in place between a rack of greeting cards and the front door, and it was this I leaned against as I looked through the display windows at Lee Avenue. The pink neon sign blinked "natiloporteM" like an advertisement for some narcotic with which we hoped to lure customers.

As I looked onto the street, I decided that I hated Beauville. After a month, I already knew what kind of place this was. Most of the boys my age who passed by the store looked as though they worked on cars every spare minute. And some of the girls were even worse. They wore neat pastel blouses, cuffed shorts, and white sandals, their hair rolled into flips or tied back into sleek ponytails, their faces at once benevolent and cunning. I knew they would all be relentless.

26

"Why don'tcha turn on that jukebox?" Val-Jean said from behind the counter. "So we won't have to sit here and listen to each other breathe."

She'd shown me how to operate the jukebox without money by turning a switch at the back of the machine. Another switch controlled the volume. When customers played their selections, Skelly sometimes came from the back room to turn down the volume if he didn't like the song.

I was tired of humoring Val-Jean. "Any requests?" I made my voice sound as flat and unfriendly as hers.

"Don't play anything stupid," she said. "I don't care what you play as long as it isn't rock and roll."

I punched the buttons for Sinatra. My mother listened to Sinatra at home.

When I was seventeen, it was a very good year.

"Shit," Val-Jean said. "What does he know?"

"He didn't write the song," I said. "He's just singing it."

I didn't know why I was defending Frank Sinatra.

Val-Jean came to the end of the counter so that we stood only a few feet apart. Her left eye was a deep blue crescent now and her right eye was puffy, as if she'd been crying or rubbing it. I was sure she'd been walloped, and wondered vaguely if her husband—a lanky, soft-spoken meter reader for the gas company—was capable of catching her off-guard with a smart right hook. I decided no.

"That song stinks," she said. "I don't care who wrote it. Frank Sinatra put his name on the label. That means he's responsible for what it says. If he's going to sing something, then he damned well better be ready to defend what it says."

"Okay," I said. I was really tired of Val-Jean now. "Let's call him up. Let's make him defend himself. 'Mr. Sinatra,' we can say, 'just what do you mean by saying that you had a good time when you were seventeen?'"

Val-Jean slowly shook her head. "Sometimes, Neva, you are so dumb," she said. She picked up a bottle of Toujours Moi from the counter and sprayed cologne along her wrists. "Let me tell you something. When I was seventeen I was working

27

time-and-a-half out at the paper mill just to keep my head out of the mud. My husband—not Sam, but my first husband Spider Loftin—you know Queen Loftin who comes in here sometimes? Her son. She's my mother-in-law. My ex-mother-in-law, thank God. I don't know who I was happier to get rid of, Queen or Spider. When we were married, Spider was working offshore, so he was home for two weeks and gone for three—though to tell the truth, him being home wasn't much different from him being gone, because he was drunk all the time he was home."

"I didn't know you'd been married before," I said.

"Ha," Val-Jean smirked. "There's a lot you don't know about me. You'll never know how much you don't know about me. I could tell you stories. But that's not what I'm saying. What I'm saying is that Frank Sinatra has no idea about what being seventeen is all about. Or twenty-one, either—all that malarky about city girls with perfumed hair. He has no idea. And you know why?"

"No," I said.

"Las Vegas," she said. "He sings all those songs like every place in the world is Las Vegas."

I thought for a minute. The song always reminded me of my mother's stories of her girlhood during World War II—the excitement of USO dances, bare legs painted to look like seamed stockings, handsome soldiers fox-trotting with girls in Augusta, Georgia one week and shipped out to a Japanese island the next.

I shrugged. "My mother's life was sort of like that," I said.

"Oh, come on," Val-Jean said.

"It's true," I said. "She's told me all about it."

"And you're probably dumb enough to believe it," she said, folding her arms across her chest in a satisfied way.

I looked out the window, where the sun made a rail glint like the blade of a knife on the railroad tracks. The deserted avenue seemed to be wavering in the exhaust of all the cars that weren't there.

Sinatra's song ended. The jukebox stopped whirring. I

looked hard at Val-Jean. For the first time, I noticed that the mass of black curls perched on top of her smooth hair was secured with hairpins.

"Is that a rat?" I said.

Val-Jean put her hand self-consciously to her head. "Oh," she said. "Sure it is. It's those birth control pills. Don't you ever take them," she wagged her finger at me. "I started up a few years ago, and now I'm addicted. And my hair's falling out on top."

"Why don't you want to have a baby?" I asked.

"I can't," Val-Jean leaned closer. She put her hand over her heart. "I've got palpitations. Sometimes they get so bad, I think I'm dying. Remember last week? That morning I was late coming in? My heart was knocking around so, I had to call the police to give me CPR."

Her eyes sparkled. For a moment, I thought she would say something more. She looked at me the way my best friend Gayle used to look when she detailed her dates with G.I.s. I was searching for the right question to ask that would make Val-Jean tell me what she knew. But at the same moment, we both became aware that Mr. Hebert was creeping down the hair-care aisle.

"Val-Jean," he said softly. "Skelly and I need some help in the back room. Would you mind?"

Val-Jean stared at him. She seemed to have lost all self-consciousness about her shiner. "No sir," she said in a loud voice. "It would be a pleasure." She glanced at me triumphantly, then headed towards the back with Mr. Hebert following.

We'd turned the volume on the Wurlitzer down low for Frank Sinatra, and I kept it down as I ran through all the Rolling Stones selections on the jukebox. There weren't many: "Satisfaction," "You Can't Always Get What You Want," "Honky Tonk Women." Cato Pruitt, the arcade man who came to change the records, knew our clientele and so kept the machine stocked with all the new George Jones,

Tammy Wynette, and Merle Haggard singles. Cato had shown me how the plays were tallied on the machine, so I played the Stones songs over and over to drive up their score.

I was standing at the window watching the 3:35 K.C.S. run through town, singing *Baby better come back maybe next week 'cause it seems I'm on a losin' streak,* and swaying my hips and shoulders in a way I'd seen Jackie de Shannon do on television the night before, when Mr. Hebert said softly at my shoulder, "Neva, could we talk with you for a minute in the back?"

Val-Jean and Skelly were leaning against the prescription counter, and when I came into the room they both smiled as if they hadn't seen me in months. Mr. Hebert indicated that I should sit in Skelly's green leatherette recliner. He sat on a high stool on the other side of the room, next to the TV. He asked me if I'd like a cup of coffee, but I told him I didn't drink coffee.

"Good girl," he said.

"Wish I'd never started up," Val-Jean said. "If I don't have my two cups in the morning, I'm not good for anything all day."

"I knew a man once," Skelly said. "Drank coffee in the morning to wake up, and drank coffee before he went to bed at night so he could sleep." He smiled his thin smile and wiped a hand over his bald head.

There was a silence, and Mr. Hebert cleared his throat. Skelly and Val-Jean looked down at their feet.

"Neva," Mr. Hebert said. "Remember when we hired you, we said we needed somebody here so Val-Jean could take some time off now and then?"

I nodded.

He looked at me for a few seconds as if to make sure I'd really understood him. "Well," he continued, "she's been doing a little work for me in my surveying business this week."

"Errands and things," Val-Jean said.

"Exactly," Mr. Hebert said, looking at her. "And so she's

been taking time off during the day when she'd normally be working here."

I nodded. "Okay," I said.

He placed the tips of his fingers together and studied them. Both forefingers were deep brown with nicotine.

"Well," he said. "It's not exactly working out. Val-Jean ran into a little trouble this morning, and it looks like she may not be able to continue doing the work for me."

"Nothing serious," Val-Jean said.

"Of course not," Mr. Hebert glanced at me. "It's just that—well, it's complicated, to tell the truth. Val-Jean's lived in Beauville all her life, she has a lot of friends in town. People who might tend to misjudge her intentions."

"I see," I said, though I didn't.

"I've been doing some surveying work out at Drew Pike's place," Mr. Hebert said. "Been working with him out there for about a year now. And times have gotten a little difficult for old Drew, so he's not been able to meet my bills."

"Gee, that's really tough," I said. Mr. Hebert clearly expected my sympathy, but I barely knew these people. I didn't know what else to say.

Mr. Hebert frowned. "Yes, it is tough. Tough for all of us. I have my own bills to pay, too, you know. Got a fine staff over at the surveying business, and they got their own responsibilities. Clifton Frazar over there, his wife just had a new six-pound baby girl last week."

"Ginny Frazar?" Val-Jean wrinkled her nose. "I didn't know that. Lord, I thought that baby wasn't due until September."

Mr. Hebert ignored her. "The thing is, Drew can't pay me in money, so we've worked ourselves out an exchange. You know I'm a quail man," he said. "And Drew's a quail man, too. So we've decided to operate on a kind of bartering system."

"You mean he'll give you quail in exchange for the work you're doing?" I said.

"Sort of," he said. "Yes, sort of like that. Only not the birds themselves, but the eggs. And Val-Jean's been collecting them for me this week."

"So after he gives you the eggs, you bring them back here and put them in the incubator?" I asked her.

Val-Jean nodded. "Yeah, only Drew's pretty busy with his cattle all day, so he said I could just go get the eggs myself from the pens."

"Oh," I said. Val-Jean's shiner was almost purple, and puffed so that her eye was scarcely open. I looked from her to Skelly, then back to Mr. Hebert. None of them would meet my eyes. "I'm not sure what the problem is," I said.

Mr. Hebert cleared his throat delicately. "Mrs. Pike saw Val-Jean out there this morning, and thought she was perhaps paying a visit of a romantic nature to Mr. Pike."

I laughed because I didn't know what to say. I looked at Val-Jean, hoping she would laugh too, but she didn't. I'd seen the Pikes together a few times in the store. He was a bent, rawboned man at least as old as Mr. Hebert; he chewed tobacco and spit the juice in a Dixie cup he carried with him. And she was monstrous—easily 300 pounds—with long black hair and a squint.

"So she's the one who belted you?" I asked Val-Jean.

"Sure wasn't the mama hen," Val-Jean said, and popped her gum.

"Ora was just upset," Mr. Hebert said. "I've known her for years, and have always thought she was one of the most charitable ladies in the world. But now she's on the rampage against Val-Jean, so it's not exactly good for Val-Jean to be doing business for me out there."

There was a brief, embarrassed silence, and then Skelly shifted slightly and said, "We were thinking that maybe you'd be able to do the collecting for us, Neva."

"Yeah," Val-Jean said. "Nobody would ever think their husband was after you."

Mr. Hebert nodded. "The birds are nesting now, Neva, so it would only be for another week or two at the most."

"I don't know," I said. "It sounds kind of scary. Besides, I can't drive."

"That's okay," Val-Jean said. "I can drive you out there. All you've got to do is get the eggs."

Fennel Road was unpaved, rutted, and covered in fine white dust that flew up from the wheels of Mr. Hebert's Impala as Val-Jean slowly guided the big car towards the Pike's. For one who seemed so reckless about life, Val-Jean drove like an old woman. The red needle of the speedometer hovered at twenty, and she drove with both hands firmly on the wheel. When I tried to talk with her, she told me to shut up.

"I can't concentrate with you yapping at me," she said.

So I looked at the landscape creeping along beside the car. The long grass grew like spears punched into the dirt at the side of the road. Insects floated lazily over the green tips that wavered a little in our wake. Here and there, the fields were broken by a farm, usually a trailer turned parallel to the road, some outbuildings, a silver silo brilliant in late sunlight, a small herd of cows watching calmly as we passed, and two or three chickens scattering back from the road. The insects popped softly against the windshield. On the steps of one of the few farmhouses, a young woman in a ruffled pink dress turned to see what disturbed the thick air. She lifted her hand to us, then turned and sat down.

The entrance to the Pike farm was at the end of the road, which I saw just a few hundred yards ahead of the trail where Val-Jean made a sharp left turn. She steered the car to a clump of pine trees, and parked in a small clearing that couldn't be seen from the road. She wiped her hands on her skirt.

"I hate driving this old thing," she said. "I'm not used to power steering. The car feels like it's flying all over the road."

"Val-Jean," I said. "What are we doing in the woods?"

"Listen," she said. "If that old bitch had been after you this morning, you wouldn't be asking such a stupid question. I know what I'm doing. The Pikes ought to be sitting down to supper right about now."

She got out of the car. "Come on," she said. "I'll walk down to the pens with you."

From the back seat she took a small cardboard box with the lid tied down with string—the same kind of box she brought from Grummacher's Bakery once in a while.

We walked through the woods in silence. Val-Jean never hesitated as we wove between the trees and scuttled through the undergrowth. She'd taken her stockings off when we first got into the car, and replaced her high heels with a pair of dirty white sneakers she produced from beneath the front seat. I had on Earth Shoes—heavy brown leather sandals that rocked me gently backward with each step. My toes were black by the time we reached the edge of the woods, and the soles of my feet felt gritty.

"You should've worn better shoes," Val-Jean pointed out.

I pushed a sweaty strand of hair from my forehead and glared at her. "I had no idea I'd be tromping through the woods after work," I said. I felt perspiration soaking through my thin cotton blouse and running in rivulets between my skin and the denim fabric of my skirt. Somehow, I'd imagined all this would be different—that the birds, being delicate, would be kept someplace cool and sterile. My face felt as if it had been smeared with Crisco, my eyes smarted, and as I slapped at the mosquitoes buzzing around my head I turned on Val-Jean.

"Where are we? This is a terrible place."

Val-Jean shrugged. "You'll get used to it," she said, looking across the strip of meadow that skirted the woods.

I could see the pens huddled there, between the woods and the fenced pasture—a squat, gray assortment of boards and wire fencing with a square of white dirt before it, surrounded by chicken wire to make a sort of cage. On the horizon I saw Drew Pike's farm, and in the nearer distance his cows were scattered like the pieces of a black and white jigsaw puzzle against the green pasture.

"This morning," Val-Jean said, "Ora Pike came swooping down out of nowhere while I was standing right here. She must've been waiting for me."

The heat created an odd, humming noise inside my head, and I was on the verge of tears. "Why didn't you just tell her you'd come for the eggs?" I said. "Why'd you let her think what she was thinking?"

"Miss Cosmopolitan," she said. "If you had half a brain, you wouldn't have to ask those kinds of questions."

She ran her shoe along the trunk of a fallen pine. The tree was rotten, and the bark flaked off in chunks that turned powdery when they hit the ground.

"I want to tell you something," she said. "And don't you ever tell a soul I said it. The only reason I ever do things like this is for what I can get out of it. And this isn't half the worst thing I've ever done. People, you know, they think they're using you. But you've just got to turn around and be sure you get more out of them than they're getting out of you."

"Wait a minute," I said. "Is Mr. Hebert paying you to come out here and get these eggs?"

"I'm not doing it for laughs," Val-Jean said.

"He didn't say anything to me about money."

She smiled and kicked at the tree.

"I don't think that's fair," I said.

"So what?" she said. "Listen, you're just a kid. You don't know anybody here in town, and nobody knows you. You think anybody would pay attention to anything you had to say?"

"About what?" I said.

"About these stupid birds," Val-Jean said. She shook the bakery box gently, and I heard things rolling around inside.

"Listen to me," she said. "This is what I want you to do. You go into the pen, and Pike's got the nests all marked so he can keep track of what's what. You go for the number two, the number seven, the number fifteen, and the number twenty-two nests. They're the nests I was supposed to clean out this morning. You take the eggs out from under the brooders and replace them with the eggs that are in this box."

A heaviness was starting to creep across my chest. I felt a pricking sensation along the back of my neck.

"What's the difference?" I said.

Val-Jean untied the box. "These are eggs from Mr. Hebert's quail. Domestic bobwhites. Drew Pike's brought in a strain from Mexico called Elegant Quail that Mr. Hebert's taken a liking to and wants to start raising."

"Elegant Quail?" I said.

"Right," she said. "Now all you have to do is switch the eggs, and then beat it back over here as fast as you can. Somebody's going to be coming after those cows pretty soon, and one black eye a day is enough for me."

She pushed the box into my hands. It bulged slightly at the bottom and was heavier than I'd imagined.

"You're crazy," I said.

Val-Jean pressed her lips together in annoyance, an expression I'd seen countless times when she was waiting on customers who were slow to make up their minds. She dug her fingernails into my shoulder and shook me twice, hard, just as the undergrowth crackled and a broad expanse of daisy-print fabric began to streak toward us from between the trees. For one frozen moment, I saw Ora Pike's red face and her mouth open in a round, astonished shape like a baby's. Val-Jean commanded me to run like hell.

I ran. Ora Pike thundered behind us as we tore between the trees. The breath ripped from her throat in great muffled gasps as her feet slapped against the path. I clutched the bakery box to my chest, pumping along behind Val-Jean. The muscles in her rump moved like machinery under the thin summer fabric of her skirt. She ran so fast that the pins slipped from her hairpiece and the rat flopped wildly from one side of her head. Following her lead, I leapt over roots, fallen branches, and puddles. Ora Pike's breath seemed to be against my neck, and as she ran she cursed and called us names. As the woods sped by on either side of me, I found myself concentrating on her words; my running became mechanical, pure motion.

She shouted, "I been waiting for you all day, I knew I'd catch you," just as I leaped over the roots of a fallen tree and almost lost my balance. Then I heard Ora Pike hit the path with a grunt, and when I slowed to look back, she was spraddled in the pine needles, clutching her ankle. Our eyes locked for an instant and she screamed, "If I'd brought my gun, you'd be two dead bitches."

Val-Jean kept the Impala at 45 all the way to the highway. She gripped the wheel so tightly her knuckles were white. My lungs ached and my throat felt caked with dust. After running so hard, I felt weightless, capable at any second of flying out the window. I crushed the bakery box to my chest.

She parked the car in the alley behind the Metropolitan. Mr. Hebert opened the back door and motioned us inside, but Val- Jean sat down on the steps and began to take off her filthy sneakers. She made him wait while she tied the two shoes together and put on her glossy white pumps.

"We didn't get them," she said, handing him the car keys.

His skin was purple; each tiny vein seemed to have a life of its own as it throbbed in his old face.

"What happened?" he said thickly.

Val-Jean pulled the last few hairpins out of her rat and stuffed it into her purse. She slung her shoes over her shoulder.

"Remind me to tell you about it sometime," she said.

Skelly now stood beside Mr. Hebert in the doorway, looking from Val-Jean to me with a nervous little smile.

"What's happened?" he said. "Neva?"

I was afraid to say anything. I was sure the moment I started to speak, Val-Jean would tell them I'd backed out.

"Come on now," Mr. Hebert rasped. "I got money tied up in this."

I was frightened by his look, and by the hard, flat way he was speaking. I figured that a confession would be better than Val-Jean's accusation.

"I didn't understand," I burst out. But Val-Jean's hand clamped down hard on my shoulder, and she gave me a pinch.

"Ora was onto us," Val-Jean said. "When she comes in

here on Monday raising hell, I'll send her back to talk to you fellers."

Her laughter sounded high and thin. Skelly looked at Mr. Hebert and then away. Neither of them said anything.

I suddenly remembered the bakery box I still clutched, and I offered it to Mr. Hebert. He immediately opened it and then his face went blank.

"Broken," he said. "Every last one of them."

He handed the box to Skelly. And when Val-Jean and I started off down the alley, the two men still stood in the doorway, looking at the eggs.

Val-Jean's scalp gleamed faintly through her coarse black hair as we walked home down streets still stifling at twilight. People fanned themselves on porch swings and called out to Val-Jean as we passed, but she barely spoke to them and walked so fast I couldn't keep pace. Finally, I stopped and rummaged in my purse.

"Here's a scarf," I said, and handed her a square of Indian cotton swirled with mauve paisley.

She shook it out and tied it over her hair. "It's a good thing Sam's out playing softball," she said. "He'd have a fit if he saw me come walking in the house dressed like this."

"What are you going to tell him about your shiner?" I asked.

She shrugged. "I don't know," she said. "I'll think of something. There's plenty of ways to hurt yourself around that store." She looked at me coolly. "Don't waste so much time worrying about these things. They happen all the time. Nobody's going to blame you."

"She saw us," I said, my voice sounding tight and small. "She looked right at me."

Val-Jean waved her hand at me, irritated. "You chickened out. She won't forget that. And I don't care—I've been paid for my trouble. I told Mr. Hebert we couldn't count on you anyways. I'm no fool. Ora Pike is his little red wagon."

We walked the last block in silence. At the corner she

turned and faced me. The shiner didn't look so bad now; it was still purple, but seemed less swollen. I thought maybe I was just getting used to it.

Val-Jean smiled. I saw myself reflected in her dark, pupilless eyes—two images, left and right, but each distinct: one locked in, the other born opposed to it and seeming to float outward. Val-Jean was moving away.

"Grow up," she called over her shoulder. "You hear what I'm saying? I'll see you Monday."

I lingered. I looked down the street at my house half-hidden behind the overgrown shrubs. On the porch sat my mother, filing her nails into perfect ovals. My father was mowing the lawn. In his T-shirt and baggy army shorts, he trudged back and forth behind the big Yazoo. His white legs looked thin and bird-like in black socks and black oxfords that were almost obscured by the stream of grass and leaves the mower spewed out. When he looked up and saw me standing there, he waved, then turned the machine at a crazy angle to do the edging.

Buddy

NEXT DOOR BUDDY HUCKABY is riding his lawn mower over the grass. Mama looks at me and smiles. The mower makes a racket under my window, choking and sputtering like it won't last another five minutes. It's been doing that since eight o'clock this morning, back and forth, right up against our property line.

"I wish he'd cut ours while he's at it," Mama says.

She sits down at my dresser and picks up a hairbrush. Mama is thirty-five years old and people think we look like sisters. Her hair is blond like mine, but curly, in a little Afro now, and it makes her look young. She wears gold rings in her ears, and we can wear the same clothes.

"Mama called this morning," she says, meaning Nonnie Rucker, my grandmother. "She woke me up. She wanted me to take her to town this afternoon. Daddy and Skip and your daddy all went hunting, and she's out there by herself. She wanted me to come pick her up right then, but I said I had to get my hair fixed at eleven and no way could I be there before lunch. You know how slow Darlene is." She pushes the brush through her hair. "God, I need a cut."

I sit up, arranging my pillow against the headboard to make it comfortable. Mama stares at her reflection in the mirror, and runs her fingers through her curls.

"What did Daddy want?"

She raises her eyebrows. "When, baby?" she says, looking at me in the mirror.

"Last night. I heard you talking."

"Talking?" Mama says, and laughs. "Talking? Huh. I might have been talking. Your daddy was raising hell like always. Coming in here at two in the morning like he had the right, demanding to know where I've been and with who." She stands and rubs her arms. "You know, it's chilly this morning. Mama said a cold front's moved in again." She looks at my bedside clock. "I've got to get a move on. Darlene wants me there right at eleven, and it's already nine-thirty. Get up now, Sherry. I've got the coffee perking, and we can have breakfast."

She goes down the hall, her bare feet making a soft, sticky noise against the tile as though she were leaving footprints. I hear her turn on the radio in the kitchen and rattle the dishes.

It's almost spring in Beauville. It's the end of February, and I imagine every place else is bitter cold. This week the Japanese magnolias began blooming all down Ferris Street, and the azaleas will be out in a month. That's all anybody ever talks about here, those flowers. They last a few weeks and that's it. The rest of the year it's too hot to grow any kind of flower.

Buddy is kneeling on his lawn, pulling trash and dead leaves from around his azalea bushes. I see him as soon as I park the car. He's wearing his blue tournament cap and smoking a cigarette. He plays golf winter and summer so he always has a tan.

"Hey, Buddy."

He doesn't say anything, just watches me walk over. A trowel and a pair of garden shears lay in the grass beside him.

"Buddy Huckaby, I'm going to shoot you."

His gray eyes are lighter than his face in the shadow of his cap. "Is your mama home?" he says.

"You know she's not home." I poke his leg with the toe of my shoe. "You talked to her when she left, not more than an hour ago. I saw you through the window." I poke him again and mimic his voice. "Is my mama home?"

Buddy teases me all the time. It's because of Mama. They went to high school together. "You're just like your mama," he'll say to make me mad.

"I guess you know Mama's taking Grandma to town," I say. "They all went hunting."

Buddy nods. "That's what I hear."

Up and down the street, the front lawns are empty. Buddy's the only one working.

"Where'd they go, out to Pine Creek?" he says.

Something in his voice makes me look at him. I don't answer, though, because there's a motorcycle coming down the street and he couldn't hear me even if I did. It's Daryl Brister. He waves at us as he races past. Buddy waves back; I don't.

"I hate motorcycles," I tell him.

"I thought you used to date old Daryl," he says. He picks up the trowel from the grass and tests the edge of it with his finger. Then he puts it down and looks up at me.

"I used to date a lot of people, but that doesn't mean I like motorcycles."

Sometimes Buddy aggravates me. He acts like he knows so much, like he knows things he hasn't got any business knowing.

"Pine Creek," he says slowly, like he's thinking about it. "Your daddy sure built a nice camp out there," he says. "Do you get to go out there much?"

"When I want to. Daddy doesn't care."

Buddy smiles and says nothing.

"Hey," I say, and pretend to be mad. "Buddy Huckaby, I'm going to shoot you if you don't stop running that mower right under my bedroom window."

He pulls a cigarette from the pack in his pocket and lights it. He hands it to me.

"It's my yard," he says.

Pine Creek is Daddy's camp. He doesn't mind me going. The truth is, I was out there last night. I have the keys. I go by myself sometimes because it's quiet and the creek is nice. Other times Mama will come. We'll take a six-pack of Dixie and drive out. We'll walk around for a while and drink. Then we'll drive home. It's not far, and it's a pretty drive once you're on the Pine Creek Road. Daddy built the camp when I was five or six years old. He's added on to it since.

Mama enjoys going out there. Sometimes she'll ask Buddy to go with her, and they'll walk around. The cabin has a sundeck overlooking the creek and the woods. Daddy uses the place mostly for a hunting camp. It's where he keeps his old army stuff, some clothes, a few of his guns, junk Mama never wanted in the house. He lived out there for a while, at first, and then he bought a trailer. He lives in town now, and goes out with a girl named Elaine. Mama can't stand her, but she's all right. She has two little boys and works at the hospital.

Last night was Ray's idea. His mother drives a schoolbus, and Mama always teases me about that. Sometimes she forgets and teases me when Buddy's there, and it makes me feel bad because Buddy's mother drives a schoolbus, too, way out in Pleasant Hill. She brings all the country kids in to school. Ray's mother's route is here in town.

She invited me to stay for supper last night, and it was afterwards when we were watching TV that Ray got restless. He started making fun of every show Mrs. Spikes wanted to watch, until she finally told him to get his ass out of her house and leave her alone.

We went riding around. We took my car because Ray likes it better, and drove around town a couple of times. Except for a few places, Beauville shuts down by five-thirty.

"I've got a couple of joints," Ray said. "Let's go out to the glowing grave and smoke."

The glowing grave is a stupid idea, but everybody goes out there. It's a grave in the Pine Creek Baptist Cemetery, and on certain nights the headstone is supposed to glow. I've been out there a dozen times and I've never seen it do anything. We sat in the car and smoked the joints, and of course nothing happened. Ray said the sky wasn't right, that he'd only seen the grave glow when the moon was full.

I was getting cold, sitting in the car with the engine off, looking out the window. I had on a sweater, but it wasn't enough.

"Let's go back to town," I told Ray, but he didn't want to. I could see my breath inside the car, and I was beginning to shiver.

"You're cold," Ray said. "Let's go over to the camp and warm up."

I'd never taken him to the camp before, but he knew about it anyway from listening to Mama. It's down the road from the cemetery, and back in the woods a little. I had to tell him how to get there, and even then he took a wrong turn. It was while we were backing out, trying to turn around and get back on the road to the camp, that we saw the other car leaving. We were too far away to tell whose it was. All we could see were the taillights disappearing down the road.

The camp is always in a mess, so I couldn't tell if someone had been there. Everything looked all right. There was even some Dixie in the refrigerator, and Ray built a fire in the fireplace. We didn't turn on the lights.

Mama has this thing about the heat, and as soon as I walk in, I have to check. The house is an oven, and it's like I thought: she's set the temperature at eighty. When Daddy was still here, they'd argue about that. Daddy finally said he was going to put a box around the thermostat, the way they do in stores to keep customers from fiddling with it. He said that was what he was going to do with Mama.

I still see him a lot. I stop by on my way home from school just about every afternoon. Daddy owns a mobile home dealership out on the Sugartown Highway, and his office is in one of the trailers. We sit in there and talk, and I'll drink a Coke or something. I think he misses us. He always asks about Mama, but then acts like he isn't listening when I tell him how she's doing. He still hangs around with Uncle Skip, and I guess they talk about us. Skip is Mama's baby brother, and he's only five years older than I am. He seems a lot older, though. He's been married a long time and has twin sons, Brad and Chad.

I guess I'd miss Daddy more if it wasn't for Buddy. We'll call him if something goes wrong. Last week Mama thought she heard someone in the storage shed, and she called Buddy. Or, he'll tell us when it's time to have the cars tuned up, or time to check the antifreeze. He and Debra had just gotten married when they moved next door. Buddy took a job at the paper mill, and Debra was a secretary at the school board. She's a nice, quiet girl, but we don't see her much anymore. Since their daughter was born, she's been staying home. Mama says Debra's got the Holy Ghost now, and spends all her time caring for little Sharon and praying.

Buddy always seems to be around. I see him working in his yard, going to the golf course, washing his car. Sometimes he'll get into his car and drive off. If I ask him where he's going, he'll say he doesn't know, or "to the moon," or something else to tell me to mind my own business. Buddy can act strange sometimes. He'll get quiet, the way he was this afternoon. Then I don't know how to talk to him. Mama does. They'll sit in the kitchen sometimes and just talk. I'll try to hear what they're saying, but I never can. It's like Buddy can hear me breathing a hundred feet away.

I'm watching him now, and I'll bet he knows it. Our kitchen window looks out onto his carport, and he's out there putting Sharon into her car seat. He's trying to fasten her seatbelt, and she's crying. She's spilled orange soda on herself. I wouldn't blame him if he slapped her, but he doesn't. He looks up at this window before he gets in the car, but he doesn't wave. After he pulls out of the driveway, I notice Debra looking out of their kitchen window. She's not looking at me, but I wave anyway.

Mama left a list of chores to do this afternoon while she's out with Grandma. It bothers me a little, but I would rather be here than downtown with them. They can spend an hour looking at one rack of blouses, or headscarves, or something else they won't buy. Grandma is still pretty, and looks almost as young as Mama, though she's nearly sixty. She even wears blue jeans sometimes.

I'm fast with my chores. Mama cleans house during the week, so I have just a few things to do on the weekends. I clean my room, do some laundry, and vacuum. Pam calls about four o'clock and we talk. We were best friends last year, but then Pam left school to get married, and now she and Randy Bordelon have a baby named Stephanie. They live with Pam's parents, and she calls me just to complain. I get tired of listening to her, and I tell her I have a lot more work to do, and that I have to go. I don't feel sorry for her. All this was her idea. She said everything would be all right, but it isn't.

I wonder how it would be sometimes if I married Ray. He's a nice boy and we have fun together, but once in a while I think of what Mama said about him when we first started dating— that I could do better. Sometimes I think that might be true, but better hasn't come along. I think about leaving Beauville when I graduate from high school, moving down to New Orleans or someplace. Daddy has family there, and I could stay with them until I found work. I could get my own place. New Orleans, though! I can't imagine living there.

Mama calls at six. "I'm having supper out here with Mama and Daddy," she says. "Don't you want to come eat with us?"

"I have a date," I say. "Ray'll be here in an hour."

"Your grandma's baked a ham," she says, knowing I won't join them. "Fresh butter beans, squash, and coconut cake. She says for you to come on out."

"I have a date, Mama."

"Be careful," she says, and in the same breath, "Have a good time. I'll be home after a while." She sounds happy.

I take a bath, and afterwards use some of Mama's Bird of Paradise cologne. She has a ton of Avon, every fragrance. And her make-up table looks like the cosmetics counter at Walgreen's. I borrow her black blouse and wear it with my jeans. She has a pair of black thin-strap sandals, and I take those, too. We'll be inside most of the night, so it doesn't matter. I even pin my hair into a bun, and wear lipstick.

Ray can't believe it when he sees me. "You look sharp," he says. He knows Mama won't come in, so he takes me right on top of my pink bedspread, with my stuffed Garfield cat looking on.

I'm at the mirror combing my hair when the phone rings. "Sherry?" Daddy says. I hear music in the background, Conway Twitty, but we have a bad connection and Daddy's voice sounds muffled. He says, "Is your mama home, honey?"

"She's out at Grandma's having supper. You can call her out there."

Ray has his jacket on and now he stands at my bedroom door, dangling the car keys in front of me, smiling.

"What are you doing home on a Saturday night?" Daddy says.

Ray's brother Jerry works nights at Sonny's so we go there for dinner. He waits our table.

"Hey Jerry, how about a free steak dinner?" Rays says.

Jerry looks around. "Shut up, Ray," he says.

Sonny stands by the steam table and he looks over at us. He smiles at me, and I wave. He's a friend of Mama's.

"Just give me your order," Jerry says. "I'll see what I can do."

After a while, he brings us a pitcher of beer. Ray grins and starts to say something about the money, but Jerry stops him.

"Shut up," he says. "It's on the house."

At the steam table, Sonny nods at us and smiles.

I'm halfway through my dinner before I notice Buddy. He must have been sitting here the whole time. He and Debra are at a table by the window, and Sharon's in a high chair beside them. Debra's hair is piled high on her head, and she's wearing a long black skirt. I can't see her face because it's turned to the window, but I can see Buddy. He's smoking a cigarette and talking to her. I watch him for a long time, but his face never changes. He just keeps looking at her, not in any particular way, and talking. It's strange and I don't know why I feel this way, but it seems pretty sad to me, the way she never looks back at him, or answers.

Ray and I are supposed to go to the movies afterwards, but
when we finish dinner I feel tired.

"Are you all right?" Ray says.

"I don't know. Maybe we better just ride around for a while
and then go home."

Ray drives my car faster than I do. I ask him to let me drive,
but he won't. He gets close to other cars and keeps changing
lanes.

"Sit tight," he says.

I know what he wants. I know he's going out to the camp
even before he tells me. He turns off the highway doing forty
and it makes me nervous. Live oaks grow next to the road,
and once or twice we pass people walking toward us on the
pavement. Ray has to swerve into the other lane to keep from
hitting them.

"Damn niggers," he says, but he doesn't slow down.

He keeps driving, and when we get to the camp he opens
the cabin door and takes me inside.

"I know what you need," he says, and begins to touch me.

I don't know how long he's been asleep, or how long I've
been lying here listening, when I finally hear the noise. It's
slight and close to the house. It might be anything. When I
was young, Daddy used to shoot deer from our doorstep, and
there are dozens of small things like possums and armadillos
that wander in.

I get out of bed and put on my clothes. I put on Ray's jacket
because it's warmer. I don't take the flashlight that hangs by
the back door. I go out to the sundeck. In late spring, when
the creek rises, I've seen the water come right up to the bottom step. The creek is low now, but I can hear it well enough.
The deck chairs are all in storage so I sit down on the banister.

It's strange how you can think you know something well,
and then it surprises you. I know the creek, and these woods,
and everything about this place, yet all of a sudden I feel like

I've never been here before. It's the shadows I'm seeing, not the woods at all. And the trickle of creek water seems to be covering up the real sound, the real noise that I ought to be hearing. I sit here looking at the woods and I'm afraid, looking out at the darkness and feeling it closing in. Then I see the man, and I know who it is.

"Where's Ray?" Buddy says to me right off. He comes up onto the deck, not walking fast, with his hands in his pockets. He has on his blue golf cap and a dark windbreaker I've never seen.

"Jesus," I say. "What do you mean by coming out of the woods like that?"

"You heard me," he says. "That's why you came outside. I watched you."

He leans up against the porch rail and lights a cigarette. For a minute, I think his hands are shaking. He's wearing a lightweight jacket for this cool night, especially out here by the creek. I'm even a little chilly myself.

"Does your mama know you're out here?" he says. He looks at me and grins.

"What brings you out here, Night Owl? Spying on me?"

He just smokes his cigarette and looks at me, grinning. He smokes it right down to the filter and then throws it, still burning, towards the creek.

"You think I'm interested in what you do?" he says.

After a while he lifts his hand and points out across the creek. "Over yonder is where I used to hunt when I was about your age," he says. "Miller's Pond, all out in there. I'd go out at daybreak, and before noon I was bringing home squirrel by the sackful." He looks at me for a minute. "Your daddy building this place changed all that," he says. "Even when nobody's out here, the hunting's not good. He's spoiled it, all right."

Daddy says this place has the best squirrel hunting in the parish, but I don't tell Buddy.

"You like to come here, though," I say. "You're always coming out here with Mama."

Buddy laughs. "It's not the same thing," he says.

"Are you in love with Mama?" I ask. I think he could say anything and I would believe him.

Buddy rubs his hand over the back of his neck and shifts his weight against the banister. He smiles at me, and then begins to laugh, hugging himself against the night air.

"When I was seventeen or eighteen years old, I thought your mama was the prettiest girl I knew," he says. "I thought that really meant something. I guess it did back then. She was like you. Tiny, though. You get your height from your daddy. Rita had the smallest hands. They were like a little girl's, her wrists not that big around." He makes a circle with his thumb and forefinger. "She was smart, too. I thought she might go off to college and marry somebody. She could have. She had an eye for that sort of thing."

"She married Daddy."

"She did," he says, "but I think you might've had something to do with that."

He acts like this is big news to me. I fold my arms around my chest to stop the shivering.

"She loved Daddy. She told me she did. She still loves him. She says she just can't live with him anymore."

"Why is that?" Buddy says. "Why do you think it is? They weren't ever what you'd call happy. I hear the way they go after each other even now—her screaming and hollering, and him slapping her around."

My mouth feels tight and dry inside. "Haven't you ever hit Debra?" I ask.

"Debra?" he says. He speaks the name like a foreign word, and shakes his head. "No. I never hit her."

"Mama makes Daddy so mad sometimes, he can't help it."

"They aren't even married anymore," Buddy says. "He ought to leave her alone. She ought to make him leave her alone. He's got Elaine, for Christ's sake. What's Elaine think of all this? Has anybody ever asked her?"

"Elaine? I say. "She's nobody serious. She's just someone he dates."

"Goddamn," he says, putting hsi face so clsoeto mine that I can smell the cigarettes on his breath. "You tell that to Elaine. Tell her how your daddy still comes back to your mama at all hours of the night. Tell her how he comes over to talk. You can even tell her that he's with your mama right now, and ask her if she minds. Don't you know I watch him? I stand there at my kitchen window and watch him beg to be let in. And every time, she lets him in." He squeezes my shoulder, hard. "What do you think it's like for Elaine? Or for me? Your mama and daddy don't ever hurt each other. They can't. They don't know how. They fight and do mean things. They even bring in other people to help them be cruel. But what happens? They don't get hurt, and never will. They're just not the kind of people who get hurt. That's why they need other people." He shakes me. "And what do you think that's like, Sherry? Or don't it matter to you one way or the other?"

I hear a faint noise from inside the cabin. For a little while, I'd forgotten about Ray, but I turn toward him now.

Buddy touches my arm. "Don't it matter?" he says.

"How should I know, Night Owl?" I ask him. "What are you doing out here in the woods instead of home?"

He looks at his watch. It has a luminous dial, and I can see from where I'm standing that it's midnight.

"You better go wake up Romeo," he says.

I start to open the door, but then turn back. Buddy's lit another cigarette, and stands watching me. "I'm sorry, Buddy."

"Why?" he says.

It's quiet when I wake up. Mama wasn't home when I came in last night; she must still be out at Daddy's trailer. Her car was in the carport and she'd left a note on the kitchen table, telling me they had things to talk about. If I'd known she wasn't home, I would have let Ray come in with me.

But he was gone by the time I finished reading the note. *It's warm this morning. The weather around here is the craziest thing, especially this time of year.*

The shades are all down next door. Buddy's car isn't in his carport, though I know Debra will be expecting him to take her to church. She can't drive.

I don't know why I'm awake so early.

It seemed a long way from town when Daddy first built the cabin. Between Beauville and the camp, there were just two small communities, two gas stations, some houses, and the Pine Creek Baptist Church. A few years ago they build a grocery store and the places grew together. Now there's an elementary school and a yellow flashing light at the intersection. It's not nine o'clock yet, but the dirt lot in front of the church is already beginning to fill up with cars. For some reason, I start looking for Buddy's car in the lot. It seems silly, but after he scared me last night by coming out of the woods, I'm a little afraid to go back to the camp by myself. I keep hoping I'll see him on the road.

This far from town, it's just woods, mostly, and once in a while, a farm. The pavement ends just past the church; for the rest of the way there's a dirt road. It's warm as April this morning, and the woods smell like cut pine.

I drive over the cattle-guard and up the path to the camp. Buddy's car is in a clearing beside the cabin, where I'm surprised I didn't see it last night. I blow my horn when I drive past the front door, thinking he'll come out, but he doesn't. I park my car next to his and get out.

Last summer when Daddy was living here, I'd drive out early on Sundays and we'd have breakfast together. He'd move the table out to the sundeck, where we'd eat breakfast and read the *Times-Picayune*. Here, the summers are so hot, the only time I enjoy being outside is early in the morning.

I keep remembering this the whole time I'm walking up the steps to the cabin. I wish it wasn't Buddy inside. I can almost feel him watching, ready to see me discover the picked lock or the broken window he let himself in by. It'll be our secret, he'll say. I lean my forehead against the door frame and listen. The woods are dead quiet; except for my breathing I don't hear a sound. I close my eyes and think about Daddy sitting in the sunlight with his shirt-sleeves rolled up, our coffee poured in two mugs on the table and the paper stacked on the floor.

Gifts

IN THE GRAY LIGHT I could make out the mattress striped in blue ticking, sheets roped against the footboard; in the night the quilt had fallen to the floor. Palmer's arm curved around his head, and as stronger light seeped in around the edges of the windowshade I saw the white mark of his absent wristwatch. His jeans and green corduroy shirt crumpled on the cushions of the chair. I stood in the doorway until he turned over and looked at me. He said my name, then I sat with him and began smoothing back his hair.

After he left I showered and dressed. I made coffee. While it brewed I smoothed the *Examiner* out on the counter. I read the news and marked the classifieds, clipped notices for immediate openings while I drank my coffee. I didn't need to call to know that each job I was qualified for would have a catch—no benefits, weird hours, bad pay. I put the clippings end-to-end along the counter and then I put them on top of each other in a neat stack. I drank another cup of coffee.

Bo-Bo jumped into the kitchen window and looked in, rubbed against the screen and tried to meow. No sound came out. He looked at me with his one good eye and waited. I raised the window, pushed open the screen, and with two delicate steps across the drainboard he was inside. I rubbed my hand down hard along his knobby spine and he flattened against the counter, purring. I felt gristle and bone under his gritty fur. He opened his mouth and rasped a meow, then closed his teeth around my fingers.

A long time ago Bo-Bo was a gray kitten with a red ribbon tied at his neck, a valentine from my husband. Missy named him, confusing the red bow he wore with the word we used for her countless small wounds. Missy's fifteen now, long-legged

59

and jittery—nothing like she was when I left her, a skinny seven-year-old curling her hair around one finger and waving goodbye from the door of her father's house.

I'm thirty-eight but no one believes it; my face is round and unlined, the face of a woman of thirty, maybe thirty-one but it's not how I looked at thirty. At Christmas when Missy was small I used to tell her about Santa: *a broad face and a little round belly,* and I'd put my hands on my stomach, ho-ho-ho to make her laugh. I'm bloated now, round the way a dead animal is round. Anyone thinks I'm pretty, it's because of my hair, still tinted copper and cut at Emporium, my extravagance.

Along with the many credit cards in his wallet, Palmer carries a California license that says he's nineteen, but when he buys liquor the clerks don't ask for an I.D. Feature-by-feature, his face is young, but I know how he fools people: he moves slowly, he thinks before he speaks, he wears an old tweed sports coat with his jeans. When he talks, his eyes cut into you the way broken glass would if you'd let it.

When the coffee was gone I spent some time on the phone; I took a nap; I washed out the bathtub. I wrote letters to people who might hire me. I fell asleep in the chaise on the patio and when I woke up, the day was over, Palmer was out of school, off work and already on his way back to me. The *Trib* came at five and I clipped more classifieds to add to the stack.

After Palmer showed up with two bags of groceries I filled two tumblers with ice and he popped the seal on the Jim Beam.

"I bought some steaks, too," he said. "And Sara Lee cheesecake for dessert."

"Fancy."

"Any luck today?"

"Kelly Girl called after you left. I worked half a day at Packard. They said they might need somebody for permanent part-time in the spring."

"That's great," he said, and we lifted our glasses. He held

the bourbon in his mouth for a few seconds before swallowing, put the glass on the counter and cupped my shoulders in his hands. "I missed you today," he said. "I missed talking to you. I spent all day potting poinsettias. A hundred-sixty-five potted poinsettias, can you believe it? They're the ugliest plants in the world. I can't figure out why people still buy them. Come January they'll be in garbage cans all over Palo Alto."

"They're not so bad," I said. "They look real Christmasy."

He shook his head. "My mother's always had poinsettias at Christmas and I thought she was the only one in the world who still bought the damned things. I figured they would've gone out of style by now."

I smiled. "That's funny," I said. "When my daughter was born I remember how surprised I was that she woke up so much in the night. People would tell me how tired I was going to be with a new baby and I thought they were crazy—talking like they lived in another century." I looked out the window, at my yard sprouting dandelions and chickweed. "Maybe I'll drop by sometime and buy a few plants for the patio." I meant this to be funny, but Palmer didn't laugh. Working at that fancy greenhouse on El Camino had convinced him I should take better care of my yard.

I rubbed my hand along Palmer's face. His cheek was rough with stubble, but across the temples the skin was smooth as a girl's. I could taste the bourbon in his mouth when I kissed him.

"I'm glad it's Friday," I said.

"T.G.I.F.," he murmured against my neck.

"The Grunts Is Free."

"Thought it was 'The Gin Is Free.'"

"That's even better. But no gin tonight. It's bourbon."

"I have to work tomorrow," he said.

I pulled away. "But I told you. Missy will be here tomorrow." I picked up my drink and leaned back against the counter.

He looked embarrassed. "I guess I forgot," he said. He folded his arms across his chest. When he did this, his shoulders hunched and he looked like a schoolboy, a kid in trouble. "Sorry," he said.

"You're afraid."

"I just don't think I ought to be here. I'll end up insulting her and she'll go back home thinking we're both a couple of jerks."

I put my drink down and took the steaks out of the grocery bag, peeled off the plastic wrap and sprinkled the meat with salt and pepper.

"Missy will like you," I said.

"She may like me, but she won't like it that I'm with you. She won't like it that we're together. She'll find a million reasons why I shouldn't be here. Whatever I am, she'll hate."

"You sound like you've had practice with this," I said without turning around.

"I know what I'm talking about."

"Well, you don't know Missy. She's a great kid."

"Carla, I used to date girls her age," Palmer said.

When I didn't say anything he left, went out the back door and into the yard. When I looked out, I saw him standing underneath the eucalyptus with the empty glass in his hand. It was December, the rainy season. The sunlight was pale on the silver leaves of the eucalyptus and on the waves of Palmer's brown hair.

When my husband filed for a divorce I wasn't thinking much about what my life would be like without Missy. There was no custody battle, none of the bitter stuff you read about in the papers. I moved out of the house and the domestic agency Scott called sent Mrs. Eakins, a woman in her fifties who moved quietly into the downstairs guest suite and eight years later, she's still there, making breakfasts, arranging dinners, taking Missy to ballet and gymnastics class. After the divorce, I went twice to the house on a whim and Mrs. Eakins answered the door. She was polite but she kept me standing on the porch.

I got a job working part-time in Public Information at a

college and that was fine, I made enough money and met some nice people. The office was cheerful, with six big windows overlooking a courtyard almost silver with debris from the huge eucalyptus trees that surrounded it. But one afternoon about a year ago I got so tired I had to rest my head on my desk after lunch; when I woke it was dark outside and my supervisor was thumping me on the shoulder. As she talked, not unkindly, about rest, detoxification, treatments that had worked for people she knew, the paper curled from my typewriter like a wave about to break, and the words I'd typed looked in danger of slipping to the floor. I kept staring at them as her voice went on and on, wondering who could be held accountable for such an arrangement of the alphabet. She said ". . . of course we'll be happy to reconsider you for the position if you'll accept treatment, if you'll only help your-self," and I realized that on the page the words were toppled together in a nonsense rhyme, the one Missy and I used to sing, *Gimby, gumby, shimble-shanks, hush-a mush-a, thimble-thanks.* I read them to the woman and her mouth closed in a hard red line. She sent me home in a taxi.

Now I spend all day at home, a bungalow in the shade of the few trees that still grow between the expressway and the creek. My husband bought me the house for his own peace of mind, he said—he wanted to be sure I had a decent place to live. A high redwood fence keeps out the neighbors, and I have the sound of traffic for company. Sometimes when I can't sleep I'll bring a pillow and quilt out to the chaise, and lie there listen-ing to the freeway noise until I fall asleep. It's a peaceful sound like the ocean, cars rolling back and forth like so many million drops of water in a narrow gray sea. When I get lonely I drive to a club near the exit ramp, and it's easy to find some-body to talk to.

That's how I met Palmer. I sat beside him at the bar and al-ready felt the warm dizziness easing through me. When I touched him he looked at me, familiar as a friend, and my face went hot in the dim light. We drank tequila that night and he wanted to talk—stories so broken and confused I took them for a drunk's ramble and stopped trying to follow. I kept watching his face as he talked—the coolness in his blue eyes, the brittle curve of his mouth, the high arch that made the nose seem a little too long. When he saw me looking at him instead of listening, he smiled as if he understood. He rolled down his sleeves and said, "Let's take a drive." We took my car. The traffic was stop-and-go and we were drunk by the time we hit the interstate. Palo Alto had been gloomy, November drizzle slicked the streets, but the interstate was a solid wall of fog. Only the spires of trees were visible here and there along the embankment.

On the beach Palmer took the kite I'd bought for Missy and the ball of twine from the back seat and began running. The fog seemed to weight the air and the kite rose only a little above his head, the red silk tail billowing with his effort. I put my hands in my jacket pockets and watched until Palmer became only a man running away and then even less, a shape being gathered wholly into the fog. I brought out what was left of the tequila and settled back against the cliff. The waves filled my head with the sound of their coming nearer and diminishing, so insistent I felt they would reach me before Palmer came back.

Hours later, Palmer's cold hands woke me in the dark and his mouth moved hard against my mouth. He said he had dropped the kite when he found the body of a seal floating in the surf.

"Suddenly I wasn't drunk," he said. "At first I thought it was a person. Then I thought it was a tire. I didn't know what it was, Carla. I kept wading farther out, trying to see what it was so you'd know."

He was soaked to the skin. I made him take off his clothes at the car and he wrapped himself in a blanket. The ocean chill seemed to have gone bone-deep for both of us. On the way home I stopped at Eddie's and bought more tequila.

Bo-Bo leapt off the hood of the car and walked slowly, loosely, as though his bones were tied together with string. He stopped and sniffed up at the steaks on the grill. He licked himself, then brushed against Palmer's ankles.

"Bo-Bo," Palmer said, squatting to ruffle the cat's ears, "you are one wretched cat."

Bo-Bo dropped onto his back, grasped Palmer's hand with his front paws and began to chew the outstretched fingers.

"You've hurt his feelings," I said.

"Some people think it's all instinct, that cats don't have feelings," Palmer said.

"What do they know?" I said. "He's showing you how much he cares."

Palmer smiled. "Yeah, sure. I used to have a cat. She was never this neurotic."

"What happened to her?"

"Dead," he said. "She had a litter when she was about seven months old, and we couldn't get rid of the kittens. I put free cat signs up at the supermarket, everything, but nobody wanted those cats. My mom finally trashed them."

Bo-Bo lay quietly in front of Palmer with his yellow eyes narrowed. When Palmer picked him up and spread him across his lap, a small cloud of grit drifted out.

"I'll get you a cat," I said. "Tomorrow. After Missy gets here we'll all drive out to the shelter and pick out a kitten."

Palmer didn't look up, but shook his head slowly as he moved his fingers through Bo-Bo's thin fur. "I don't want it," he said. "It wouldn't do any good." His shoulders under the blue shirt looked rigid, and he held himself so completely apart that for a minute I felt that I was sitting alone in the yard. But when I leaned over and touched him, Palmer was real, solid. I tousled his hair.

"Oh well," I said. "Doesn't matter. I forgot your mother. I guess she hasn't changed her mind about cats."

"She hasn't." He looked at me steadily. "Make me feel better," he said. "Say something."

I rattled the bits of ice in my glass and held it out for a refill. "Dame Trot and her cat led a peaceable life, when they were not troubled with other folks' strife," I said, remembering a nursery rhyme I used to tell to Missy.

Palmer laughed. "Tell me how you got Bo-Bo," he said.

"A gift," I said. "He turned out to be a nice gift, too, but I didn't think so at first."

"Whose gift?" Palmer said.

"What?"

"I said, whose gift? Who gave him to you?"

I put down my drink and got up to turn the steaks. "Scott always thought I needed things to take care of. He gave me plants, an aquarium, the cat, you name it."

"Missy."

"Sure. Her too."

"Did you love him?" Palmer said.

I bent down over the grill. "That's a good question," I said. "I used to wonder about it sometimes myself."

"Doesn't it bother you?"

"That I've stopped wondering? No, of course not."

Palmer leaned back in his chair. "Does it bother you that I want to know about him?"

The coals were white and my face felt warm from the heat. "It's okay that you asked. I don't miss being married, if that's what you're after."

"It isn't. I mean, it is, but I'm asking something else, too. Look, there he is, some fancy doctor who lives in a fancy house with your daughter, and here you are with me."

"So?" I looked around. "There are worse places to live, believe it or not. You've lived a sheltered life if you think it can't get worse."

"That's not the point."

"No? Then what is?" I sat down and picked up my drink.

"Listen, don't get mad. I'm just—I don't know, curious or something. I mean, here we are together. We make love, we have some good times, a few drinks, what have you." Palmer rocked his chair down and rested his elbows on his knees. He looked a little drunk; he cupped his chin in his hand and stared at the rainwater puddled around the roots of the eucalyptus.

"And?" I picked up the bottle of bourbon and poured another shot into both our glasses.

He took the glass and held it. "It's like—well, you know when I'm with you, when I'm inside you, say, and I look into your face I feel like the woman I'm with isn't you at all."

"You *are* drunk."

"Don't make jokes. I'm trying to say something. Right now, talking to you, it's hard to believe you're anybody's mother, that you were ever anybody's wife. But other times that's all I can see about you."

I shrugged. "Maybe that's your problem."

He looked up, then ducked his head and smiled. "Probably."

I liked to look at him like that—his shoulders in the work shirt were broad, and he held his head down and a little to the side, sheepish. It was such a boy's face; I could imagine it in the stupor of its childhood sleep, eyes closed and lips parted, one hand open on the pillow. But then Palmer stretched his legs onto the chaise, nudging against me. The soft suede mocassins he wore were so old the stitching at the toe had broken, just at the point where his big toes pressed. And I remembered that under the washed-out corduroys his long legs were tan and muscular, warm when he wrapped them tight around me.

What could I tell him of all those years of fidelity and loneliness? I imagine there are days—maybe weeks—when Missy and Scott forget me. I'll be waiting at an intersection, or filling out a job application, or even making love, and I remember that I have a child somewhere, a daughter who was pulled from my body fifteen years ago, whose first words I listened for, whose hands I held between my own and taught to hold a spoon and wash themselves. And I wonder why that wasn't enough—what in me was so impatient that I couldn't bear her childhood out? But before I know an answer, the traffic light will change, my number will be called, the man holding me will cry out my name in the darkness.

"Marriage," I said. "It has good points and bad, like everything else. I just married the wrong person. When you do that, a part of you goes a little crazy after a while. You start wondering who you hate more—yourself for getting into such a fix, or the other person for not being what you want."

Palmer shook his head. "I can't feature being married," he said.

"Oh, come on," I said. I smiled at him over the rim of my glass. "You'd make a terrific husband."

"Yeah?"

"Sure," I said. "You'll see. Someday you'll find somebody nice and it'll be fine."

He looked at me for a few minutes. Then he shook his head. "You don't know what you're talking about," he said.

The wind rifled the leaves of the eucalyptus and kicked up dust in the yard. I sat in the chaise after dinner with a quilt tucked around me. We had run out of ice an hour or two before and the bourbon tasted warm and smoky on my tongue. Palmer sat in the chair beside me, drinking. He'd put on his tweed jacket but his hands trembled around his glass and I asked if he was cold.

"I like winter. I like cold weather," he said. "When I was a kid, we spent New Year's at Tahoe. Snow and ice. Chains on your tires. In Tahoe it gets really cold. Colder than this."

I pulled the quilt tighter. "Maybe. I'm not interested in winter. To me it's something finished, there's nothing to wait for anymore. I like fall—just when the air begins to look different, bluer, and the leaves start to change." I thought for a minute. "It's a lot like making love."

"How?" he said.

"What I like best is knowing it's going to happen. I like that feeling of inevitability more than the sex."

"You're a little crazy, you know that?" Palmer said, and sipped his bourbon.

"Well, the sex is okay, too," I said. "With you."

But then he didn't want to talk about it. He bent his head and wobbled his glass slowly on one knee.

I felt we'd been drinking for hours, but now Palmer didn't seem drunk at all, only difficult to focus on. Bo-Bo came slinking out of the bushes and jumped onto the chaise. He nuzzled at the quilt, and I turned back one edge to let him climb under.

"My old pal," I told him.

Palmer looked over at us. "You could do anything to that cat," he said. "He might bitch, but give him ten minutes and he'll be back rubbing himself on your leg, wanting to be friends again."

"He gets lonely," I said.

"Or hungry."

"Maybe to him they're not so different." I pushed the quilt down and reached for my glass.

Palmer didn't say anything, his face didn't change. He lifted his glass to his lips and set it down again without drinking.

I took another drink and said, "Listen. I want you to meet Missy. She looks just the way I looked when I was her age, but she's nothing like me. You can tell by the way she dresses—even her jeans are ironed." I pulled up the quilt to show my wrinkled pants. The zipper was unzipped and my underwear showed. "Nothing fits me anymore. I used to wear a size 8. Can you believe it, with this belly? My skin's bad now, too. The color, I mean. It looks sallow against my hair. My hair's the only thing about me that still looks decent, and that's only because I pay somebody to keep it that way."

"Carla," Palmer said.

"It's true," I said. "I used to be a lot better looking."

"You're still pretty," he said. "You'd be prettier if you took better care of yourself. You gave Bo-Bo half your steak."

"I eat when I'm hungry," I said. "I don't get hungry anymore. I don't know why I'm so goddamned fat. I can remember when I was nursing Missy. I had an appetite like a truck driver and I never gained an ounce. I'd wake up in the middle of the night to feed her and end up having eggs and toast or a sandwich before I went back to bed. I liked those nights. She'd look almost drunk lying in my arms. But if I moved her, even the slightest way, she'd wake up and begin to feed. And then she'd doze off again."

I watched Palmer lift his hand to his cheek and rub along his jaw. "How did you lose her?" he finally said.

I picked up my drink. "Like a glass slipper. Like a hen that lays golden eggs. You name it. It's just the same."

"No," he said quietly. "It's not. I mean, that night in the bar, you drifted in and you said the right things. I liked it. I needed you. But I could've been just anybody sitting there. And what if I didn't need you? Would that have been it? One night getting drunk together, a fuck on the beach, then nothing? I mean, how many times have you done that, Carla?"

I looked for his face coming out of the shadows. "Well, you weren't just anybody," I said. I tried to look at him more closely—wanted to see if the expression on his face was anything like what I heard in his voice—but either the bourbon or the darkness kept me from it. "Meeting you in a bar has nothing to do with Missy anyway," I said.

"Then why don't you have her?"

"Maybe I didn't want her. Or maybe Scott wanted her more."

"He must have loved you," Palmer said.

"Well, he was wrong."

Palmer poured more bourbon into his glass. I was beginning to feel the drinks, and the cold wind against my face made me sleepy and uncomfortable. I wanted to stop our talk, to go inside and make a place for myself in the bed and sleep until I didn't feel bad anymore.

"So I'm the terrible one," I said, to end it. "But living with him was terrible too. Even this is better. At least I don't have to apologize to anybody for the way I am. I can do what I damned well please. I call my own shots here."

Palmer seemed not to have heard me. "That night in the bar," he said. "That first night. It was like you were coming to

me from some place we should have always been together. I
was so strung out that night . . ." he rolled his glass between
his palms and looked to me. "I don't know," he said. "When
I came in from class that afternoon my mother was there with
her boyfriend—she was in this little robe, and he had on a pair
of swim trunks. And he kept telling me how wonderful it was
that we have a pool. I started thinking about my old man,
how he wasn't really so bad, you know. You'd look at my
parents together and see nothing, just a regular couple. But
what was between them must have been hell. My old man
never got over it. Even when he was dating a chick with big
boobs and driving a white Porsche, he couldn't understand
why my mother had 'done that' to him. And he always saw it
that way—when she started going out, it was something she
was doing to him, it was a personal attack. He died four years
ago. Had a heart attack on a sales call—keeled over in somebody's reception room."

I reached for him, touched his knee and almost fell out of
the chaise. "Listen," I began.

He steadied me. "Doesn't matter," he said. "Another story,
another night. I was talking about something else."

"The bar."

"Right. So finally, the guy left and my mother and I started
talking. In about five minutes, she was raving. She told me if I
didn't like her life to get the hell out, and started screaming
that Dave—Dave with bikini trunks and the rank after-
shave—was the only person who cared for her, that I've never
loved her, that I blame her for the divorce, for my father's
death, for my crummy grades in school, the whole works.
When I walked out, she was throwing things into the
pool—books, dishes, clothes, stuff out of the refrigerator. She
said she'd drown herself."

"Would she?"

Palmer shrugged. "This happens about once a week. I keep
thinking I'll get used to it. When I left the house I didn't want
to see anybody. And then an hour later there you were. I
mean, it's so damned random. I could have gone to another

bar and met someone else, or I could have told you to get lost."

"Maybe you should have."

In the silence that followed, Palmer came to sit beside me on the chaise. His face looked brittle, and his pale eyes were hollow in their sockets.

"Why can't you just be what I need?" he finally said. When I didn't answer he put his hand under my chin and turned my face toward him. "You're not Missy's mother. Not anymore."

"You're right," I said carefully. "She's been without me half her life. We don't have much in common anymore. When she's not here I try not to think about her. I don't want her to exist for me unless she's standing in the same room."

Palmer's hand tightened on my chin. "What does exist for you?" he said. "This crummy little neighborhood? That god-forsaken cat? Any loser who comes by wanting a fuck?"

I pulled free of his hand. I wanted another drink very badly. I wanted to lie down some place warm, not to talk anymore. I felt around on the ground beside the chaise for my glass. I found it, but when I went to pour in more bourbon the bottle was empty. Then suddenly Palmer was taking things from me—the bottle, the glass, the quilt finally—and as he weighed me down with his body he said so softly that he could almost have been talking to himself, "You love me. Say it. Say you love me."

When I woke it was still dark, and I lay on my side with my face pressed into Palmer's chest. The cold night air bit my shoulders and I pulled up the quilt but it wasn't large enough to cover both of us. I moved my hands underneath Palmer's shirt, along his ribs, and he stirred a little, his arms tightening around me. The smell we gave off was whiskey and the sweet, grassy smell of sex, and it lay so lightly around us that it seemed almost a part of the night.

For a long time I listened to the noises rolling in from the freeway. A car sped by out front and I heard a man yell "Hey Carla! Car-la-a-a-a!" over the fading noise of its radio. Palmer

mumbled something and I stroked his face lightly, soothing
him back to sleep. He huddled close. I don't remember waiting for the night to pass, but when I opened my eyes again the
trees over our heads hung their leaves into fog and everything
around us was the air getting colder.

Measure Twice

CHRIS KNEW SHE WAS STARING but had no inclination to stop. She was fairly sure the men couldn't see her anyway—she was inside the glassed-in porch, and they were across the backyard, adding a new room to the Millers' house. The Millers' baby was due any day now, and though the addition to the house was to have been completed weeks ago, spring rains delayed the work. The men assigned to install the exterior siding had arrived only that morning.

The men had already been working for an hour when Chris came out to the porch for breakfast. She worked at home in the summer, and liked the casual routine that evolved once her spring classes ended: she rose early, showered, dressed, then ate cold cereal with her coffee while she read the newspaper. By 8:30, she was in front of her computer. She told the few colleagues she encountered in the department mailroom that her study of poetry was almost writing itself, and though she didn't say it, she felt certain that its publication would secure her tenure.

At breakfast she brought her cereal and mug of coffee out to the sunporch. The tiny glass box of a room had been added on thirty years ago, when Chris was in kindergarten six states away, but it was exactly the kind of room she would have added if she'd owned the house then: just large enough for a small round table and two chairs. Her houseplants flourished in the filtered light that shone through the branches of the tall maple trees, and between the plants she could look out on her small, neat backyard, separated from the Millers' by a low board fence.

She spread her napkin into her lap, then glanced up and saw one of the carpenters stripping off his shirt. He was young, but at this distance he could have been any age from eighteen to about twenty-five. As he pulled up his shirt, Chris could see that his chest was hairless and tanned, and that his nipples were dark brown. He was tall and muscular, but unlike the other men working around him, his body also seemed supple and lean; where the other men's muscles were knotted or bulky, his were smooth flat planes.

In the split second before he pulled his head free of the shirt, Chris had already caught herself. I'm as bad as my students, she thought—the women who talk about men as bods and hunks. At different times in her life Chris had had three lovers, but even with Isaac, whom she'd truly loved, Chris had thought very little about their bodies, and usually tried to avoid looking at them naked. Their hairy pouched bellies and sunken chests seemed as pathetic and vulnerable as her own flaccid breasts and dimpled thighs, an embarrassing secret they now shared.

The carpenter pulled his shirt free of his head, shook back his hair, and Christina felt a pang of lust so keen, it embarrassed her. Except for his clothes—he wore only a pair of belt-less, faded jeans and sneakers now—he could have been one of the sweet-faced Amish farmers she sometimes glimpsed on the long weekend drives she took alone in the country. His hair was long—it would have fallen below the collar of a shirt, if he'd had one on—and a shade of brown so light it was almost blond, though the color seemed to her more interesting than blond, richer, less predictable. When he pushed his hair back, Chris saw that his face, too, was different from the other men's: he had a long, sharp nose, thin lips, high cheekbones, and he wore round, gold-rimmed glasses.

As she sat staring, she decided it was the contrast between his muscular body and the intelligence in his face that made him interesting. With that face, he could have been one of her graduate students. That he was, instead, measuring long planks of vinyl to nail to the Millers' house, and had acquired his strength along with his skill—well, how unlike her students, who were so often pale, and already a bit puffy around the middle. This man worked carefully, measuring and re-measuring before he made the cuts, then methodically fitting and shimmying the siding into place. The other men talked together, smoked cigarettes, scratched their bellies, but he worked silently, his hands deft and sure. He seemed totally alone out there, oblivious to the men, to the whine of the power saw, to the rock music on the radio, oblivious even to the patches of morning sunlight that played so gently against the side of the house where he was working. As she lifted the heavy blue mug of coffee to her lips, Christina felt the stillness of her own house behind her like a presence.

She rested her elbows on the table and watched the carpenter walk inside the Millers' new room; she could see his silhouette occasionally pass by the window. Perhaps, she thought, that is why I fell in love with Isaac; though he was older, he had a quality that the men my age lacked.

As always, when she thought about Isaac, she felt a deep, numbing sadness, sometimes indistinguishable from bitterness, that began in the center of her chest and radiated outward. Isaac was erratic and forgetful, a little vain about his age, but he was also brilliant—even now she found herself repeating ideas he'd provided in his own lectures, and when she caught herself she'd blush, and stumble over her words, and she knew the students probably interpreted this as a young professor's lapse in confidence. Isaac had been her lover for five years, while she finished her coursework and wrote her dissertation. And it was his recommendation, Chris knew, that had landed her this job. She thought how he'd teased and taunted her into making each chapter perfect, how he goaded her into publishing articles, how—after an evening spent dissecting theories of poetry—they would make love on her fold-out couch and lie in each other's arms until the magic hour of midnight, when Isaac would rise, and dress, and go home to his wife and teenaged children.

The carpenter stepped back into the yard, and Judy Miller followed him. He crouched to point to the bottom edge of the siding, and a band of untanned skin appeared between his tanned waist and the top of his jeans. Chris imagined tracing her finger along that white band, feeling the fine grain of the skin beneath her own skin; she tried to imagine how he would turn to her when she touched him, what combination of muscle and bone and intellect would finally push them together and transform him into a man with a history, an appetite, an aptitude, a man whose eyes were blue or green or brown, a man whose name would be like water to her parched lips. She closed her eyes, thinking, and when she opened them, the man was standing, explaining something, moving his hands to mimic the line of the house, and Judy listened, hands on her hips, her enormous belly like a boulder between them.

As Judy waddled back into the house, the carpenter turned away; he picked up a thermos bottle and drank straight from the mouth, then recapped it and picked up another piece of gray siding. As he nailed it above the last completed row, Chris saw in every gesture how completely he'd dismissed Judy—he had a job to do, and Judy, though she was cute and blond and didn't look thirty-five, was only the middle-aged woman who'd hired him to do it.

Chris looked down at her watch; ordinarily she'd have started to work hours ago. I'm wasting time, she thought. But she continued to stare as the man worked. Even at a distance, Chris saw that his face was serious, young, intent on perfection. As he stood back, making sure the rows of siding were even, he smoothed the straight, lank hair from his forehead. Chris felt a familiar sadness as she watched him, as she recognized how badly she wanted to touch his forehead, to let her hand trace down his lean face and across his shoulders. It was the feeling she used to get in class, when she watched Isaac lecture. Though she took notes and answered questions, what she felt was the distance his marriage imposed on them— his averted glance, her downcast eyes, the perfunctory nod when the seminar ended.

Chris knew she could just open the wooden gate between her yard and the Millers', go in on some pretense and strike up a conversation with the carpenter. She would hold his gaze, stand close enough to smell the sweat that he had just now wiped from his forehead. But what would they talk about? What would she say when he looked at her—at her body already spreading and softening with age, at her face already faintly lined? Nothing she could say in a few minutes would interest him, she understood that. She felt suddenly powerless, empty, old.

She walked to the window, rested her hands against the sill, and watched him work. Row after row of siding went down over the plywood, and Chris knew that by tomorrow the job would be finished. The carpenter worked hard. When he turned his head at certain angles, the sunlight glinted off his glasses, and though he sometimes glanced toward her house, if he saw her there he gave no indication. She wore a blue tee-shirt, khaki shorts, sneakers—the same kind of clothes she wore in college, where Isaac had touched her face and said that at no other time in her life would she be so beautiful.

Thanksgiving

MY WIFE JEAN HAS HER BACK TO ME and walks down the beach toward the water. The cuffs of her dungarees are rolled up around her ankles and her loose white sweater moves with the light wind. It is late November, and everything is dull gray. The boards of the porch and the sand that blows over them are the same color as the water and sky.

The house has been closed since summer. It has been here at the end of Lafourche Parish for years, gradually wearing out, beaten deeper every year into the sand. The front windows are large and low, and standing before them, I can see the familiar span of sand and water. These three large rooms are seldom warm, and they smell of the Gulf and old furniture. My mother was here last, sweeping, mending, zipping on the white slipcovers against the damp air. She hasn't come here for the holidays since my father died. She says it is too lonely, and bad for her arthritis. Only the warm months can attract her. In summer she calls and leaves messages at my office: "I'm going to the old house this weekend, Will. Don't you come down." And so I don't. I come back in the autumn to find a few things changed—a rug removed, a lamp broken or replaced, heavy white pottery mugs instead of the blue china ones. And I leave my own alterations: a cane chair bought for the porch, a shelf of secondhand books from a shop in New Orleans. Jean has added her grandmother's white quilt, tattered and sprigged with violets in an old pattern, and a small reproduction of a Bonnard interior which hangs over the kitchen table. It is the only ornament in this house full of discarded furniture.

It has rained all morning. We woke early and lay in bed a long time without talking. Jean knotted her fingers through mine and drifted in and out of sleep. I smoothed her dark hair over her shoulder and listened as the rain beat into the waves. I thought about nothing. The air smelled damp and full of brine, and I wanted to get up and go outside. She woke when I moved, her eyes wide and inquisitive, and pulled me to her. I didn't want her. Her mouth had the same salt taste that I smell now on the porch.

The sand is packed and wet, littered with grass and bits of garbage. She has leaned over to roll her pants up to her knees and seems bent in half, her long legs planted firmly into the sand. Her shoes lay abandoned on the bottom step of the porch, the socks hanging from them carelessly, bright as tongues.

She walks down the beach with a rapid, distinct stride, the way she might walk a city street. Her head is up, lifting her face into the spray, and her hair makes a dark streak down the back of her sweater. The waves move against the blue of her dungarees. After a while, I quit watching and turn back to the room, which lies quiet now without her.

After our coffee this morning, Jean pulled off her long white nightgown and went in to shower. I watched her swollen image in the mirror as she wound her hair into a bun. In the kitchen, I unwrapped the small blue hen that would be our dinner. Jean has never cared much for cooking, and she likes it even less now that she is going to have a child. I prepare most of our food, simple meals of meat and bread, green salad and wine. I stuffed the hen and was lacing it up with large, loose stitches when Jean finished her shower. She came into the room wrapped in a towel, smelling of sweet soap and toothpaste.

When I did not speak, her voice rose on its familiar impatient note. "I told you I'd do that," she said. She was combing her hair, watching as I cut small chunks of butter and placed them over the bird, then sprinkled the skin with herbs.

I covered the hen with tinfoil and put it in the oven. The low heat was already beginning to take the chill off the kitchen, but my glasses fogged as I leaned close. At the sink, Jean rinsed the cold coffee from her cup with a sharp twist of her hand. The cup clattered into the sink and she walked back into the bedroom.

I sat down at the kitchen table with a book open before me and looked out the window. Behind the house lay a hundred yards of sand and beyond that lay the highway. I watched a long time but no cars passed. It was quiet except for the thud of raindrops against the roof. An hour went this way, perfectly still and peaceful. Jean came through the kitchen once, but I did not look up as I heard her go into the living room and set-tle on the sofa. Perhaps another hour passed before the rain seemed to let up and I heard her throw down her knitting and go out, the screen door slamming behind her.

We have known each other for so long that I cannot pay at-tention to her moods. They are hard and black, but they leave with the same swiftness with which they come. In the living room, her knitting is strewn over the sofa, a soft, pastel mound. Last night when we left our apartment on the West Bank, it was the last thing she put in the car. She spread it carefully over her lap and knees, and I heard the click of her needles before the city had receded in my rearview mirror. She has trained herself to work without light, and did not even notice when the pale orange lights of the expressway gave way to a black country road.

I no longer see her through the front windows or the screen door. I believe that I come to this house now to escape the monotony of our square white apartment, which lies with others in a raw development just west of the city. Jean maneuvered us there, perhaps believing that our uneasiness with each other was due to the deteriorating house on Dumaine Street where we spent the first years of our marriage. The house was worn and white with pillars and a bay window, an exaggerated frill of woodwork framing the porch. Upstairs there were several stark, asymmetrical rooms we did not decorate or even use. There are no extra rooms in our new apartment. The white walls and wood floors give the illusion of space. The rooms are very small, and we are never far away from each other when we are in them.

Yesterday morning, hours before we left to drive down here, we received a Thanksgiving card from my sister's four- and five-year-old daughters. Alice's large block printing filled the inside of the card. Beneath her name, my sister had printed in Katie's in small letters, and had then written "Just wait until you have two!" I would like to call and ask her what she means, what we should wait for, if all things must come in pairs, but she would only laugh at me as always and hand the telephone to my mother.

I have wondered how it would be to live here alone. I imagine how the days would pass into other days, and I can see the rooms as I would have them, clean and still under square white patches of sun. I imagine walking the mile up the highway to Landry's store for groceries, and rising early to drink my first cup of coffee in the dark kitchen.

Seven or eight years ago, when I was in college, I came here alone for the weekend. Jean was visiting her family in Lake Charles, I think, or maybe we'd had an argument. This was before we were married. I got drunk on Friday night, sitting on the beach with a bottle of scotch my father had left in the house. All Saturday I slept and nursed the hangover. In the evening I drove to Grand Isle for a seafood dinner. I bought drinks for a girl at the bar whose small black eyes seemed to disappear farther into her tanned face as the night wore on. We danced a broken two-step across the linoleum until I was out of money and the girl's brother came to take her home. I woke up late on Sunday and drove back to school without stopping for breakfast. My car had a flat tire outside Napoleonville. It was September, but still hot as hell.

The rain has beaten the sand into a pocked pattern of gray and darker gray. Jean's footprints are barely visible as they veer sharply down to, then away from the water. The beach is empty and quiet. So much has not changed in the nearly thirty years I have known this place. The house next door, empty today, is still painted yellow. A peeling boat sits beneath the high screened porch. The first night I brought Jean here we lay under the boat with a six-pack of beer. We could see my parents moving around inside our house, getting ready for bed. We drank beer and kissed, and then we made love for the first time, though Jean was afraid of my parents' shadows and the small noises that came from around us. In the morning my father and I took a walk on the beach while Jean and my mother made breakfast. He asked me if Jean and I were "serious" about each other, and I said I supposed so. He smiled as if everything were settled. But it was several years before Jean and I were married.

Jean is clear-eyed, pretty in a healthy way. Her face pleases me the way my own might if I examined it closely in a mirror. She has a fine, strong body which has leaned a little awkwardly into pregnancy, and a wide, soft smile, which I do not see often anymore. But when we were first together she was very happy and light, and when she smiled I knew that we must love each other. I had never been in love with anybody before and neither had she, and when for a short time she believed there would be a child we began to talk of marriage. Then there was no child, but the talk continued, and at the end of it we were married. We moved into the house on Dumaine, which had once been owned by her relatives. She was happy and when I read or wrote business letters upstairs in the evenings she did not complain.

She had never lived in New Orleans before and she thought the city was exciting. It was not until later that the house became too large for her, and then the city became too dangerous and sad and we moved. She explained to anyone who asked that the house had been too difficult to heat and to furnish.

This house, too, is difficult to keep warm. The Gulf sprays the windows with mist and a fine, corrosive salt. Even the furniture we bring here loses what little shape and newness it has retained, becoming so colorless and worn that I no longer bother to remove the white slipcovers. The pages of the book I have been reading feel soft and pulpy from the air.

In Jean's bag there are skeins of blue and pink yarn, which she is knitting together into a kind of tweed covering for the baby, and a book on child care. I put her shoes down beside the bag and turn off the light in the living room. The rain has begun again, but lightly this time, and the room is dark.

Jean is moving up the beach. She walks slowly with her head bent, and stops occasionally to pick up a rock or a shell, or to look out over the waves. She jumps away when a big wave breaks, and once I see her throw a rock into the water just as it begins to curl. She must hardly feel the rain.

I watch as the window screen becomes patterned with tiny, colorless dops, and feel a sharp wind rise. It is near winter. She is walking more quickly now, and from the kitchen the rich smell of our dinner drifts in over the darkness.

Field

WHEN DAVE BOUGHT THIS HOUSE, the neighborhood went: our street, the field, then ocean. That lasted one summer. The condominiums went up across the waterfront, and we walled in our deck for the privacy. Three years went by before anybody bothered about the field.

A work crew is out there breaking ground. The yellow Caterpillars roll back and forth, levelling the earth in wet black rows. What's left of the field is just turning green again, so that the new grass is thin and brighter than grass should be. It looks like cellophane grass you'd put in an Easter basket.

Nelda asked me didn't I mind new houses going up at my back porch. She bought a place inland, where the houses are already on top of one another. She was here the day the surveyors arrived, and we stood on the back steps to see what they were up to. She touched my arm and said to think about the field as ordinary ground, something for people to build on. She said it was nothing but space, and when the houses were built the field would be space filled up and forgotten about. "Even so," she said, "it's a shame they're building right up to your back yard." I've known Nelda since grammar school. We were in each other's weddings, and she is Jen's godmother, as I'm godmother to her Andy.

When I was growing up, no one thought about building houses before there were people to go in them. Somebody wanted a house and it was built. Nobody called this beach a resort then. When Dave and I first moved out here from town, people didn't come here on vacation. I guess that's what we were thinking when we moved in. We were thinking about hurricanes when we should have considered how things can change. I miss seeing the ocean every time I look out the window. Dave won't say.

Jen was always full of the devil. I'd tell her not to leave the yard, and then she was two blocks away on her tricycle, playing with children I barely knew. "Mama," she'd say, "I can take care of myself," when she was only four. I know every yard on this island, but things are different now. The day Jen disappeared, I began looking for her the same as I had a dozen times before—my mind on what I'd make for supper that night, irritated with her for wandering off. I looked for her tricycle, and called her while the light faded from the streets and the beach began to grow dark. Nelda kept naming all the places Jen might be, and we'd look and she wouldn't be there. She wasn't in the field then, either. The police said she wasn't in the field until three days later.

Andy and Jen were born just a few months apart. He sits on my lap and spells for me off cereal boxes and the bread wrapper. He counts to one hundred. Nelda starts him into kindergarten next fall. He could have gone this year, but Nelda said she wanted him home a little longer, that she was in no hurry. She had the option.

Before our babies were born, Nelda and I would make up stories about them, planning how they'd be. From the beginning, Nelda wanted Andy to be a boy so she started watching football games on TV with her husband and talking to me about Cub Scouts and Little League. I always knew Jen would be a girl. In those days, my thoughts of what she would be as a child got mixed up with what my own childhood had been. I saw a little blond-haired girl playing on a dirt road in the sun, and didn't remember that the road was paved while I was in high school. She wore pinafores my mother sent to Goodwill years ago, and shoes of a style no longer made.

When Jen was born, she looked like Dave; she had the same curly brown hair and his green eyes. Sometimes, watching her play, or holding her as she slept, I was surprised to see that she resembled me at all. I had gotten used to the idea that she was Jen, and not the little girl I'd imagined before her birth. She would cut her doll's hair and then cry because it wouldn't grow back. She was a tomboy who tore around the neighborhood in overalls and sneakers but fussed to dress up on Sunday, looking at herself for hours in the mirror. She would flirt in her own way, putting her arms around Dave's neck and laughing. His eyes would search for mine over the top of her head and his expression would say, "This is something, isn't it?" It was a look familiar to me from the time Jen was a baby, bundled into the soft pink or yellow sweaters I'd knitted, and he would trace over the network of veins still visible beneath her thin curls as if his fingers were searching out a pulse.

When Dave came home the night Jen disappeared he said, "Don't tell me she's off gallivanting around?" His thin, tanned face looked tired and a little worried, but mildly, as it had that night when Jen was a few months old and her fever rose suddenly before breaking. Dave laid his jacket down on the table and walked back through the front door and into the street with me following, and Nelda with Andy in her arms. He held me by the shoulder and said, "You're barefoot, you've been running around out here with no shoes. You'll hurt yourself."

"Take her back into the house," he said to Nelda, "and fix her a cup of coffee." I watched him walk down our street. He looked so sure he would find Jen playing out of earshot that it seemed he was on his way to the next block to pay a visit. And later, when the police had gone, and we were lying awake in the hot darkness, he said, "What were you doing? Didn't you miss her earlier?" As I sifted through the small events of the afternoon he began to cry, holding me, his head feeling as heavy against my breast as a child's body.

The kids used to play in the field because it was safer than the street and the grass was high. It was a jungle when the game was army, a forest when the children were playing knights. It was safe. We'd spot jack rabbits out there in the evenings, and once or twice a year somebody would find a nest of field mice or an armadillo. I don't know who owned the field. Nelda said she heard it belonged to a family in Atlanta and was finally sold to settle an estate. After the kids found Jen, nobody played in the field the rest of the summer. Gradually, I began to see them come back. A little boy would run across the field on a a dare. I'd see them standing around the place where they'd found her, a grave so hurried and shallow that it hid her body for less than a day. Their fear began to wear off. The kids were playing in the field just as they always had, until the surveyors came and the land was fenced. Their mothers tell them, "Something bad happened to Jen. Somebody hurt her and she died." These women are my friends. Their children played in the field again but not without somebody always watching. "You can't make a child stay inside," the women tell me. "But you can watch." I listen for the accusation of negligence in their voices, expect it.

It was months after Jen was found, and the coroner had examined her, that Dave and I could turn to each other again. This is difficult to explain. When Dave would touch me, I thought of the violence of what had happened, and the image of Jen being so badly used was hammered into my mind until I would have to leave the house to get away from it. Dave would find me walking on the beach, or sitting in the sand, waiting. I wanted to be vulnerable, to have the stranger approach and try to drag me back into the dunes, to try to touch me as he had touched Jen, so that I could begin to slash at him with the filleting knife I'd carried with me from my kitchen. Dave would hold me until I had stopped crying, and then we would walk together past the row of condominiums, past the black field to our house with its porch light on.

We talk now and then about buying a place in town, and renting this house during the summers. We drive around the old part of town, looking at the basketball hoops nailed up over garage doors, the white-washed fence dividing each house from its neighbor, and though we don't talk I can tell that Dave is thinking as I am—that Jen's death may not have happened in these places.

We drive back to the beach, talking about what we would have to move out of our house if we rented it, and how the same. But it's more than that. Moving back to town would be denying what's happened, would be like starting over again as though Jen had not been born.

I wonder who would rent this house now, with the construction going on behind it. Nobody will pay to watch that. The crew has measured off the lots, and a geography of water mains and electricity is already mapped. And the developers carry around a portfolio of house plans. I've seen their ads in the paper; they've given out a number to call. They know the people they're looking for.

When I think of Jen, I see her life as four neat squares, like lots, or pages from a calendar. Inside each square I arrange everything I can remember: a pink-flowered dress, "Here we go round . . . ," transparent blue glaze of the tea set fitted inside a wicker basket, our trip to the Everglades. I look at photographs we took and think not "three years old" but "the summer before she died." I had film in my camera when she disappeared, and the police developed it for a photograph. I'd taken one the day before, of Jen standing on the beach. When the local news ran the photograph the second day she was missing, one of the men from Dave's office taped the broadcast on his video and gave us the cassette. "You'll want to remember this," he said, because he thought nothing terrible could happen, that just like everything else on TV, Jen's story would work out fine.

I used to walk with Jen along the beach in the early afternoons. We were looking for shells, unusual pieces of seaweed, and tiny, ribbon-striped rocks to string and hang in her window, mobiles for the wind to catch. We often saw men on the beach, strangers who would sit against the dunes drinking beer, the heels of their boots dug into the sand. It was always the same. The beach would be nearly empty. Jen would run barefoot along the edge of sand where the surf pulled back, and she hollered when she found a shell she liked. Her voice would carry back to me and I was thinking always of something else, or talking to Nelda, who sometimes came along. On those days, Jen and Andy would compete, traffic in town is heavy, and the neighborhoods all look the each trying to find the best shell, and calling on me or Nelda to judge.

The day that Jen disappeared, we had returned from the beach, and the children went into the field to play. They were hiding from each other, and when Andy went to look for Jen he couldn't find her. I was standing on a kitchen chair while Nelda pinned up the hems of my new pants. Through the screen door, I could see him walking towards the house slowly, stopping now and then to look at something he'd found in the grass. That moment is precious to me now and seems frozen, the last moment of not knowing, with the sun in a haze over the field and Andy coming through it, a small boy in a blue shirt and jeans. And then he presssd his face against the screen and asked if Jen was with us, he couldn't find her anywhere. Nelda looked up at me and then stuck all the pins she'd held in her mouth back into the pin cushion.

The summer heat made Jen prone to rashes so I rubbed her several times a day with baby powder. As Nelda and I walked the neighborhood that afternoon looking for her, it seemed I could smell the powder on each turn of the breeze, rising up sharp and sudden the way the salt smell of the ocean will. I thought about Jen as she'd been that morning, wrapped in a towel, watching me run her bath, the water warm and bubbles added so that she could sit there and look at comic books until her skin shrivelled. I remember her brown curls, short and frizzing a little around her face from the humidity; her tanned legs; the small feet planted on the bath mat; her impatience later when I made her stop to dry off carefully, as not to leave wet footprints down the hall.

Nelda says another child will come when the time is right. She says this with her hand resting on Andy's head, her voice sure of itself and her authority. She sees me watching Andy sometimes and always makes a point to say, "He's grown up faster than a weed!" as she reaches to pull him to her. I sometimes pass the time thinking what it would be like to have a son huddled warm against me, his mouth wet all around with milk and fallen open, the newborn hands clenched tight around nothing. But I'm afraid of a morning when the child will wake and look at me as I stand over his crib, and what I will see will be not his face, but Jen's, the way it was that day in the field, her eyes half-closed and dried blood caking her nose and chin where the man had kicked her, and broken her neck like an animal's.

I turn my hands palms-down on the porch rail and see the aging, though I am still young, only twenty-seven. I've lived for years in this place, facing the ocean; my skin stays brown right through winter. When I carried Jen, the skin on my belly stretched as she grew, and the silver marks sprang up vivid as tattoos beneath my tan. I felt my body was too small to hold her, though she was not a large baby. Nelda had read that unborn babies like their mothers to talk to them, and so all that summer I would lean back on the steps in the evenings, talking to the baby about what I could see ahead of me. I would put my hands around her as she lay kicking, and tell her about the field, the last sunlight reflecting off the water, someone walking down to the beach. I'd sit like that, holding her and talking, until we both could sleep.

Still Life

FROM THE OUTSIDE 2441 Avenue de Ursulines looked no different from the other historic buildings in the Vieux Carré. The pale peach eighteenth-century stucco reflected so much light that Emily, standing on the sidewalk, had shielded her eyes as she read the polished brass plaque highlighting the building's history: in another century, it had been a school, an orphanage, a hat factory. By 1900, it was only an apartment house, but by the late seventies, artists had converted some of the apartments into studio space.

Emily searched for the buzzer and, finding none, turned the knob of the street door. It swung open, and in the long interior corridor, the first door on the right was Bennett Jackson's. Emily tapped gently on the smudged white muntin, and when she received no answer, rang the bell. I must be early, she thought.

Twenty minutes later, Emily watched the street through the dirty panels of glass framing the front door, and pictured the thick red braid swinging down the middle of Bennett's back, the wooden soles of Bennett's scuffed blue clogs as they clattered on the cobblestones. Then a chestnut horse trotted past, pulling a tourist cart, and Emily felt the first stab of knowledge that she was being stood up, abandoned in a city she knew only from childhood trips at Mardi Gras.

She turned and looked behind her, hoping to see Bennett walk down the hall wiping her hands on a paint-smeared rag, a cigarette bobbing between her lips, her head tilted quizzically to one side as she shoved out her arm for a look at her errant wristwatch. But the hall was empty, a conduit open to the outdoors at the end, divided into one band of shadow, one of light. Inside, where Emily waited, the plaster peeled away from the wooden walls and the rich, dank smell of decay hung in the humid air. A fungus, rusty as old blood, spotted the as-bestos ceiling tiles, and the wooden floor sagged and creaked as she shifted her weight.

Emily reminded herself that though she'd made the telephone call, it was Bennett who'd suggested they meet for lunch. "You've never been to Galatoire's? Then we'll go there," Bennett said, and Emily was flattered, a little giddy after weeks of telling herself that the older painter wouldn't have time to see her. They'd met at an artists' colony the summer before. Bennett was guarded, and though Emily never allowed herself to think she'd gotten close, she was pretty sure Bennett liked her. They ate dinner together often, and one evening in Emily's studio, Bennett had admired the drawings Emily made of the wild grasses she'd found in the woods. They stood silently at Emily's table, Emily still marveling at the easy juncture of stem arcing into flower, the leaves folding over each other like hands, the articulated white blossoms so ex-quisitely ordered, yet each different in the subtleties of growth.

"Cleavers? Is that what you called this? It's what we always used to call goosegrass," Bennett had murmured, tracing one finger above the pencilled lines of prickly stems and leaves. "So delicate and . . . ," she caught her bottom lip between her teeth and studied the drawings. ". . . and so slight, really." Bennett turned her yellow-flecked blue eyes on Emily, and the two women stood there under the lamp light, scanning each other's faces for a moment before Bennett smiled, and Emily, unsure what to say, unsure what she'd been told, slipped the drawings back into her portfolio. As the women stepped from the studio into the cool summer night, Bennett pressed her hand and said, "Strange, isn't it, the way our subjects find us?"

Bennett hadn't singled anyone else out for her attention. Though their paintings were nothing alike, the women had both been born in Louisiana, they both kept a garden and they both had children, and in that way they felt set apart from the group, whose talk was generally about movements and theories and making connections—talk which Bennett said bored her, but which made Emily feel anxious, as if the small fruit and flower paintings she did weren't enough, as if paintings like hers could hardly matter in the world these people talked about with such confidence and contempt.

Sometimes these people said Bennett was crazy, though Emily never understood if they meant crazy in the insane sense or just unusual. "Real Southern Gothic crazy," a sculptor explained, but Emily, being a Southerner herself, didn't know what he was talking about. To Emily, who lived now with her son and husband in a small Midwestern university town, Bennett seemed one of the sanest people she'd met in a long time. At the end of the summer, Bennett said, "Look me up if you're ever in New Orleans," and Emily promised she would.

But now Emily began to wish she'd never left herself open for this. After all, Bennett had a reputation for unreliability. Bennett herself had told the story of forgetting so often to pay phone bills, electric bills, tuition bills from her children's expensive private schools that her husband hired a part-time secretary. And Emily had laughed, agreeing she was guilty of the same fault when in fact she was so obsessively reliable that Matt called her his little bookkeeper.

I must have said something wrong on the phone, Emily thought. Something stupid that made her reconsider.

She thought about a column she'd read in the newspaper over breakfast: a reader had written to The Word Wizard asking if "funny" could be correctly substituted for "odd" or "strange." Emily read The Word Wizard at home, too, and though she was pretty sure he'd been wrong once about acceptable colloquial usages of the verb "to fix," she still winced at his no-nonsense reprimands to people like her, who misused the language.

At a party last week, Emily had told an art professor that Bennett's work had taken some funny turns in the last decade, and her stomach clenched as she remembered the man's smirk, his knowing grin. She hadn't understood then; now she heard his mental correction: she should have said "unusual."

What I fear most is true, Emily thought as she stood scraping her fingernail over the flaking paint along the door frame: I'm not an artist. How can I call myself an artist? People still treat me like a kid, or worse, like a hobbyist, promising-young-Matt's-wife-who-paints. In her head she replayed the little dramas: Oh, you paint? Isn't that nice, well my wife paints, and my daughter and my mother and sister and aunt and the next door lady, too, all so busy at their easels . . . and as her face stretched into smiling, Emily could all but see the raging seascape, the weathered barn, smug pink roses in a translucent vase with an armor of highlights over the surface, glittering until her head felt ready to burst.

All I have ever wanted, she thought as she looked at the faded green paint crumbling under her nails, is to see things for what they are. No one expects a cornflower to be a cosmos, a peach to be a lemon slice if only you dig deep enough. What I love is a great rosy lump of peach against the spiked petals of a cornflower such an aching shade of blue it seems a trick of nature, a tiny, perfect celebration, Jubilee Gem.

She ran her finger down the pane, leaving behind a smudge of clean glass, outside color bleeding in bright. If Logan were here, she thought, he'd write his name.

But her son was at this moment on a riverboat ride with his father. Matt had skipped the afternoon program at the geography conference to give her this time with Bennett.

"Don't worry about it," Matt said that morning in the hotel, when she apologized again for making him miss the lecture. "Nobody goes to them all."

But the lecture this afternoon will be the important one, Emily told herself, the one everyone will be talking about at the party tonight and for weeks afterwards. And it's my fault he's missing that lecture, though he won't admit it.

Emily looked at her watch. I shouldn't have come, she thought. Even if Bennett does show up, we'll have nothing to talk about. It's been too long. I should have written to her, should have tried to keep in touch. She'll say: what are you working on? to be polite, and I'll try to tell her, but when her face goes blank with boredom I'll get nervous and won't finish my sentences. So we'll talk about the food, about how humid New Orleans weather is. Then she'll ask about Logan, and we'll wind up talking about our kids. She'll tell me about all the places Logan must see while we're here. Then she'll suddenly remember someplace else she has to be.

Emily turned back to Bennett's door and frowned at the name scrawled on a yellow Post-a-Note above the doorbell. The casualness of making that square of paper serve as a nameplate, even of the racing, disconnected letters of Bennett's name in black, felt-tip ink, gave the whole enterprise a temporary, slapped-together feeling, though Bennett's studio had been here for years. Emily rang the bell again. Maybe Bennett was on the phone, or working on one of her huge, vehement paintings. Emily sat on the stone step in front of the studio door and pulled her skirt down over her calves. Mosquitoes hummed in her ears and small, itching lumps sprang up along her ankles and bare arms. The stone was cool through her thin cotton skirt; she was glad she'd chosen a dark print that wouldn't show dirt. Cigarette butts and scraps of paper littered the splintered wood floor of the hallway, and as she looked up at the tangle of pipes branching over the opposite wall, a huge black roach darted behind them. She pulled her feet closer to the step and tucked her skirt tight behind her knees, but then immediately she stood and began to pace the creaking floors.

At the opposite end of the hall, the floors were brick instead of wood and sunlight played over them. Emily walked past the closed doors of other apartments, past the stairwell where bags of pungent garbage mounded against the iron staircase to the second floor, and entered a tiny courtyard overgrown with Confederate jasmine and firethorn.

The air was cooler in the courtyard; though October sunlight beat down from the square of sky overhead, Emily felt the faintest breeze stir her long skirt against her legs, and she pulled her wispy, dark hair up off her neck, wrapping it into a bun that would unravel the moment she took her hands away. She'd been away from Louisiana a long time; since her parents died, she'd no reason to come back, and had forgotten the awareness of body that the humidity forced. Down here, she was a different person, always a little wild-haired and disheveled, a little damp, not quite in control of how she looked. In Maine, she and Bennett said that Louisiana was *sensual, torrid, fecund*—three words they'd laughingly agreed on one chilly night over Bennett's scotch. But now Emily remembered why she'd been so eager to leave, why she alone of her sisters had insisted on going away to school. Living in this humidity again, she decided, would be like living in a jar of mayonnaise.

The foliage banked between high walls of rose-colored brick gave off a sweet, earthy smell that Emily had thought inseparable from the decay and the garbage she'd been smelling since she entered the building. The brick floor of the courtyard was almost entirely taken up by a rusting black wrought iron table and two chairs. On the table sat a chipped blue mug and a blue plate where two sandwich crusts embraced a shred of lettuce, and three green flies crawled over a bitten yellow apple. Emily stood for a moment watching the flies, close enough to see the threads of their black legs mincing over the creamy flesh of the fruit, browning now at the teeth-marks. Something gripped at her heart, made her mouth water; the apple lay open in quarters, each one seeded with a star, each bitten only slightly, ruined. She let her hair fall hot and limp around her shoulders, and looked around at the closed doors lining the dim hallway. From behind one of the doors came the noise of a TV game show; from somewhere else a persistent, hacking cough. Emily heard gospel music and women's arguing voices. Everyone seemed to be here except Bennett.

Emily walked up the hallway and back to Bennett's door. She felt almost angry being here, angry at the heat, the squalor. She rang the doorbell again, hoping Bennett might have come in while she was in the courtyard. In the silence that followed, she sat down on the step and rested her head on her folded arms.

Bennett is married to a well-to-do doctor. They own a house in the Garden District and a summer place on Lake Pontchartrain. Why play the artist here, in a musty building with exposed pipes and roaches, that's what I'd like to know, Emily thought. Clearly Bennett has never had to *live* in a place like this.

She thought about her own studio, a small, bright room on the bottom floor of her ranch house, with a view of the patio and the flower garden, a room with her favorite postcards tacked up over a worktable and clean brushes in a Chock Full O' Nuts can. This summer, with both Matt and Logan home from school, she'd worked while television noise drifted down from the living room and the typewriter clacked in Matt's study. Privacy meant that Logan and Matt were not allowed to come into the studio, but when they wanted her, they called from the top of the stairs.

And I answered them, Emily thought, as if I could be like Bennett, who has everything, three children and her paintings and a husband who hires people to make sure the bills are paid and supper's on the table at six o'clock sharp. But when I answer Logan and Matt, it's the beginning of the end of my working day: Logan's bored, or Matt wants me to read an article he's working on, or to help him look for something.

She scratched her arms, stood up, and rang the doorbell again.

Down the hall, a door banged open and a woman shuffled onto the bricks, pushing herself along with a cane. Sunlight from the courtyard made a nimbus of the white hair around her head, a silhouette of her narrow body under the loose dress. She carried a paper grocery bag. Emily watched her come closer, afraid the woman might be startled to see a stranger in the hallway. Emily rang Bennett's doorbell again, coughed, and folded her arms, tensed for the moment when the woman would speak.

Waiting for someone? she figured the woman would say, and heard her own hesitant, dull reply: Yes . . . Bennett Jackson . . . this is her studio, isn't it?

And the old woman, shaking her head, would laugh: Miz Jackson! She's always late. . . .

The woman's sleeveless sack dress, printed with pink tulips on white polished cotton, had a bold border at the hem like a curtain. She meandered toward Emily in flat black slippers crushed down at the heel and thick white athletic socks striped green and gold at the tops.

I should leave, Emily thought. I should walk out, I should wait outside for Bennett, who's now (she looked at her watch) forty minutes late. But waiting on the sidewalk would be worse, I'd feel like a fool and the mosquitoes are even more vicious out there. Matt and Logan are supposed to meet me back here in an hour and a half, she calculated. I could leave. This is New Orleans! There must be someplace interesting to go. Haven't I read the guidebook? I could go to a cafe, for a cup of coffee (she thought of herself, alone at a table near the back, feeling conspicuous); I could take a walk through the French Quarter (if she disappeared in New Orleans Matt would never know where she'd gone, she could be abducted and dismembered and no one would know where to begin looking for her, she'd be dissipated like fog, gone without a trace, a tragedy Logan would live with all his life and it would be her fault, the lapse in her good judgment).

"Hey," the woman said. She stood in the middle of the hall now, near the stairs, halfway between Emily and the courtyard.

She probably thinks I'm a junkie, or a prostitute, Emily told herself. "Hello," she said, smiling.

"Hot day," the woman said, gesturing vaguely with the hand that held the sack.

"Yes," Emily said, wondering if she should ask the old woman where Bennett had gone.

"I said, is it hot enough for you?" the woman called.

"It is," Emily said.

The woman tossed the sack into the stairwell and leaned on her cane, staring at Emily. "You like the heat?" she said.

"Not very much. I—"

"Me neither. Awful heat. My fan's broke."

"That's bad timing," Emily said, conscious that her voice sounded insincere. Why can't I relax? she asked herself. She often fantasized about meeting interesting people—people who would tell her their life stories, whose faces would imprint themselves on her memory while she waited for the bus or bought groceries—but this had never happened, and Emily suspected that interesting strangers could probably intuit the lack of sympathy her tenseness brought on, and confided in someone else instead.

The woman approached Emily. Her narrow face, the color of yellowed linen, had probably once been pretty; the cheekbones were still high and delicate, and her pale blue eyes were lit with a crafty look. "You ever fix a fan?" she said.

Emily blushed. "No, I—well, my husband usually takes care of things like that."

"Your husband," the woman said. "Where's he at?"

Emily stared at her, trying to decide whether to launch into the truth, or if she could get away with less. "He's not here," she said. "But he'll be back soon."

"Oh," the woman said. She seemed deep in thought, wobbling the tip of her cane over the splintered floor. "You can't fix my fan?"

"I'm afraid not."

The woman tapped her cane on the floor. "Well," she said. "Then looks like you're no use to me."

From down the hall a woman's voice bellowed "Alice! Alice Wolff!" making the name echo off the high cracked walls.

"Theona," the woman said, jerking her head in the direction of the voice.

"Alice Wolff!"

"Is she calling you?" Emily asked.

The old woman stuck out her bottom lip. "If she wants me, she knows where I'm at. Didn't she say, 'take out that trash?' "

A dwarf in a filmy green nightgown stepped into the hallway, shook her head tiredly, and began to walk toward them. The woman's body looked like a magician's trick, an adult's head and body fitted with a child's limbs, and despite herself, Emily stared. Tight black ringlets curled around the woman's wide face, and her blunt features gave her a testy look. She wore no make-up, but orange polish frosted the nails of her hands and bare feet. "Alice," the dwarf said when she reached the two women. "I have been calling you."

"I ain't deaf, Theona," Alice said.

"Then why didn't you answer?"

"I asked this woman can she fix my fan."

"Can she fix it?" Theona jerked her thumb at Emily.

"No, she says her husband can."

"Where's he?"

"Gone off somewheres," Alice said, waving her hand into the air, as if to indicate the vast space Matt might have disappeared into.

"Just like a man," Theona said, hands on her hips. She spread her little feet out and looked Emily up and down, a faint smile playing over her wide mouth. "Has Alice been bothering you, lady?"

"Oh no, I'm just waiting for someone," Emily said. "Someone who works here." She put her hand on Bennett's door, flat out. All three of them looked at her hand, long and bony, with its two gold rings and a diamond on one finger.

Theona said "huh?" or "her?" but Emily wasn't sure which, and the dwarf's brooding face made Emily reluctant to ask her. Emily let her hand drop from Bennett's door and Alice took it up in her own knobby hand, saying, "When your husband comes, you think he'd mind fixing my fan?"

"Alice Wolff!" Theona said.

Alice shrugged. "I asked you nine times and that fan's still broke," she said. "You ain't going to fix it, Theona."

"You can fix yourself some ice tea. That'll cool you off," Theona said. "Come on back inside."

"Rude," Alice said. "Sometimes I think you got no more manners than the man in the moon." She held Emily's hand so tightly that a knot of panic began to rise in Emily's chest. Emily smiled at both women and tried gently to pull her hand away, but Alice held fast.

"Do you think she'd ever say please?" Alice tugged at Emily's arm. "No ma'am. It's do this, do that. Bossy. That's Theona's middle name."

"Lady," Theona said, turning her face up to Emily. "Have you ever seen such a big old girl acting this way?"

Emily looked from Alice down to Theona, and they both looked back at her, waiting. She cleared her throat. "Do either of you know Bennett Jackson?" she said.

Theona brushed at the yoke of her nightgown, fingernails scratching at the nylon. "A whole lot of people stay in this place," she said. "Half of them won't give you the time of day if you ask for it."

"I ain't never going to get that fan fixed," Alice grumbled. "I'll be dead and gone and still be sweating to death." She squeezed Emily's hand, and at the release, Emily pulled her hand free.

"Do you have a phone?" Emily asked Theona.

"Yes ma'am, we do," Theona said.

Alice took Emily by the elbow, tugging her close. "When Wal-Mart put their phones on sale for $6.99," she whispered, "we snatched one up."

The apartment Alice and Theona shared was miserably hot. Dark green shades, pulled down to the sills of the huge windows, flapped listlessly in the muggy breeze. As Emily dialed the number at Bennett's summer house and let the phone ring and ring, she looked around the room; it was big as her airy studio at home, but layered in heavy antique furniture, dark carpets, thick drapes. A mahogany four-poster squatted in the center of the carpet, flanked by an iron cot on one side and a long, polished dining table without chairs on the other. The broken fan—an ancient black iron oscillating model, with blades like the blackened petals of a flower—sat wrapped in its long cord on the table top. A marble-topped washstand inlaid with blue tiles across the backsplash hunched beside the kitchenette where the phone sat, wedged on the lip of the countertop between cans and boxes of food. With one slight tug on the cord, Emily felt sure the phone would crash onto the floor. Alice ran water in the kitchen sink, fussing softly about the heat, but Theona sat on a low stool beside the table, obviously listening. Her short legs stuck out straight, the way a child's would, and she stared as Emily held the receiver to her ear.

The black woman who answered on the ninth ring said that Mrs. Jackson wasn't home, and when Emily asked if she knew where Bennett was, the woman said, "I reckon your guess is good as mine. Who's this?" Too embarrassed to leave a message, Emily hung up the receiver and shouldered her purse. "My friend must be on her way," she told Theona, and reached into the small front pocket of her bag. "I'd like to pay you for the phone call," she said, holding out a quarter.

Theona knocked her feet together and laughed, and Emily noticed that the toes looked gray and gritty. "Lady," Theona said, "You owe me a hundred dollars."

"Excuse me?" A hot blush began to rise on Emily's throat. These women are crazy, she thought, trying not to panic. She continued to smile and hold out the quarter, staring into Theona's sharp black eyes.

"A hundred dollars is what I'd charge you to use my phone," Theona said. "But since I'm not charging, you can have that call for free." Alice cackled, and Theona said, "Turn off that water and quit laughing at every little thing I say."

"Bossy," Alice mumbled, but she turned off the water, and dried her hands on a dish towel. She took some jars from the refrigerator and pushed the phone carelessly to one side, making room on the counter.

"Well, thank you very much for the phone call," Emily said. "It's very kind of you."

"You're very welcome, I'm sure," Theona said, and grinned. She held out her hand, and when Emily took it, Theona scooted forward and pulled herself off the stool. "Do you like our house?"

Emily looked around, confused, wondering if there were other rooms, and said in what she hoped was a cheerful voice, "This room is very nice."

"One big room is all there is," Theona said, and pulled her over to the washstand. "My great-great-grandma up in the Felicianas had this washstand made. Slaves built it right on the plantation. 1859. That was the year she married my great-great-granddaddy. Alphonse Mouton?" Theona squint-ed at Emily, as if she expected a response, then ran her hand over the dark wood. She held her clean fingers up for Emily to see. "Alice keeps a nice house," Theona said. "Have you been to the Felicianas? Have you seen those houses up there yet?"

Emily, who'd visited plantations in the Feliciana Parishes on interminable Sundays when she was a little girl, and now wanted to explain nothing about her life to these women, simply nodded. "It's a lovely piece of furniture," she ventured, and touched the cool blue tiles, though she wondered if it was as old as Theona said. I look naive, Emily reminded herself, and this woman has gotten it into her head that I'm a dumb Yankee tourist. I just hope she doesn't try to sell it to me.

Theona tugged at her hand, and when Emily looked down, the woman's face was so full of concern that Emily felt a sudden pang of guilt for doubting her; it was a wise face, sober and maternal. "Honey, are you hungry?" Theona said.

"Yes," Emily said, and looked at her watch. "I'm supposed to meet my friend for lunch."

115

"Friends like that, you'll starve to death," Alice said from the kitchenette. "Theona and me was just about to have dinner. I'd be happy to make you a sandwich."

"I'm sorry," Emily said. The heat made her dizzy, and she was beginning to get a headache. "My friend will be here any minute. But do you think I could have some water?"

"I think you could," Theona said.

"Thank you," Emily said. "And then I really have to leave. My friend might come back while I'm here, and she'll think I've gone."

"That'd be a shame," Theona said. "After you waited such a long time."

"Cheese, bread, mayonnaise," Alice said. "What else now? Let me know what I forget."

In the courtyard Alice cleaned off the table, grumbling about their filthy neighbors. The flies rose lazily off the dishes and resettled almost immediately when Alice set the plate and cup down outside a closed door.

"Crazy old thing," she whispered to Emily, pointing at the door. "Can't even hold her water half the time. Pees all over herself."

Standing beside the table, Emily nodded glumly, clutching a metal tumbler of iced tea that Theona had insisted she take instead of water. Sweat beaded the outside of the glass and dripped down, splotching her dark skirt.

"Sit down, sit down," Theona cried, dragging her wooden stool into the courtyard. "I brought my chair." She pushed the stool up to the table and sat down, then motioned Emily to take the chair beside her. "Sit down, now. Make yourself comfortable."

While Alice hobbled from their apartment to the table, bringing paper napkins, china plates with chipped silver rims, two more metal tumblers, a cut glass pitcher of tea, Theona cut the crusts from the sandwiches and swept them into her palm with the knife blade. When Alice sat down, she handed the crusts to her.

"Birds'll like these," Alice said, and dumped the crusts into a napkin. "I just love the birds," she told Emily.

"Alice had a parakeet once upon a time," Theona said. "But he died. Are you sure you won't have a sandwich?"

Emily shook her head. "You're really kind to ask," she said. "But as soon as I start eating a sandwich, I know my friend will come in."

"Serve her right," Alice muttered, chewing. "But you're missing out on a treat. This is Velveeta."

"It looks good," Emily said. Thick layers of cheese stuck out from between pieces of bread so fine-textured and white that Emily had, at first, not known what it was.

"Now listen, honey, you can't tell me no," Theona said. She put half her sandwich on a napkin and pushed it over in front of Emily. "Half a sandwich never spoiled an appetite. You eat that."

Emily lifted a corner of the thick, gummy bread and peered at the cheese before taking a bite. "This cheese is the color of marigolds," she said.

Theona laughed. "Marigolds," she said. "Now that's one flower that stinks."

"Long time ago," Alice said, brushing crumbs from the top of the metal table. "I used to work for Theona's family. Theona's mama had marigolds in all the windowboxes of their house on St. Charles."

"They stunk then," Theona said. "They still don't smell so sweet to me. Honey," she said, addressing Emily, "when my mama died I took that apartment in there and I've lived no place else since."

Emily chewed her sandwich and nodded. "You must like it here," she said.

"Like has nothing to do with it," Alice said. "Theona's family cut us off. Her sisters is all married to lawyers and what-not. They give us some of her mama's furniture, though."

"That's worth something," Theona said. "I told you that before." She smoothed the silky green fabric of her nightgown over her breasts and looked down thoughtfully at her plate. "When Alice was young," she said, "let me tell you, she was beautiful. She was like a storybook girl, all blond and rosy. And you'd be surprised at the men I attracted. My sisters, they figured I didn't need to go out, didn't need to marry, being like I am. Believe me, I could have married if I wanted to, any one of several. But Alice! Well, my sisters had themselves some second thoughts about Alice."

Alice cleared her throat and touched Emily's wrist. "In 1937," she said, "I was the Swine Princess."

Emily smiled uncertainly.

Theona waved her hand. "She's still talking about that," she said. "Good God, I was just a girl then. Didn't even know Alice Wolff."

Alice pursed her lips. "The Swine Festival is a big to-do," she said. "Was then and it still is." She tapped Emily's wrist again. "My daddy, you see, was a farmer."

Theona took a bite from her sandwich, then scrubbed at her fingers with her napkin. "Honey," she said, "Alice Wolff came from Basile to New Orleans in 1940 with two dresses and a nightgown in a paper suitcase. I still remember that thing. My mama put it up in the attic, and I'd go up there and stare at it, wondering that there was such a thing as a paper suitcase."

Emily looked down at her glass. A fly crawled around the blue rim and she brushed it away with her finger. It droned off, then circled back and lazily began to crawl across the table. "What kind of work did you do?" she asked Alice Wolff.

"Oh, different things," Alice said. "Lady's maid, mostly. That's why Mrs. Mouton wanted me for Theona. Somewhere, there's a picture of us outside the Cabildo." She turned to Theona. "You had on that green hat?"

"That day on the river," Theona said. "I remember." She poured more tea in all their glasses, then laid her hand gently over Alice's. "We go back a long ways."

"Your friend," Alice said, turning her wrinkled face to Emily. "She's somebody special to you?"

Emily sighed. "I don't know." She rubbed one hand down her cheek. "I thought she was," she said. "She was nice to me a while ago. I liked her. We had things in common." She thought about the drawing of the cleavers she'd made, about Bennett's finger tracing over it—a stubby, calloused finger, short-nailed, blunt, a shadow on the white paper.

"Tch," Theona said. "You never can tell what's on peoples' minds."

Alice leaned forward and patted Emily's knee. "Don't go feeling bad about yourself, now," she said. "Could be anything kept that lady from coming. Car trouble. Man trouble. Maybe she's a drinker." Her hooded blue eyes flicked to Theona, then back to Emily. "One time I had a friend," she said. "Sweetest person you'd ever want to know in this world. Do anything for you. Give you the shirt off her back when times got tough. But if you counted on her to be where she said she's going to be, count again."

Emily pressed the sweaty metal tumbler of tea against her cheek. "Why?" she said.

Theona clapped her hands. "Alice Wolff, you and your stories," she said. "You're going to get yourself in hot water."

Alice gave Emily a sly look. "Distracted," she said. "She'd set out to go one place and forget where she was headed. Get side-tracked. I'd walk past the old market and there she'd be, half an hour after she's supposed to meet me for coffee at the Morning Call. You know what she's doing?"

Emily shook her head.

"Drawing pictures," Alice said, and laughed.

Emily turned to Theona. "Do you paint?" she said.

Theona shrugged. "Honey, everybody in New Orleans paints," she said. "Dime a dozen. You've been down to Jackson Square?"

Emily remembered the rows of sidewalk artists, their repetitive sketches of pretty, lace-trimmed balconies and palm-bedecked courtyards. "Sure," she said.

"Theona never did paint pretty pictures, though," Alice said. "She made wild things."

Theona tucked her napkin under her plate. "That was a long time ago," she said.

"Do you still paint?" Emily said.

"No, honey," Theona said. "Heart's gone out of it. If you don't feel that fire, then there's no use making marks on the paper."

Alice pecked at Emily's knee with one bony finger. "Snakes. Cantaloupe rack down at Ma Anthony's. Big Lucille in her underclothes. Things nobody'd want to see anyway."

"You see what I mean?" Theona said to Emily. Her face was set, the lines deep and her mouth drawn down at the corners. She smoothed the corner of her napkin carefully. "Alice didn't like me looking at the world so much."

"I told you those pictures was dumb," Alice said.

Emily touched Theona's arm. "I'd like to see your paintings," she said.

"Honey," Theona said, stripping off the corner of her napkin and balling it between her fingers, "they went up in flames."

"I burned every one of those ugly things up," Alice said, waving her hands out wide, showing the fire. "Right here in this courtyard. Big oil drum fire."

Emily looked at the old woman's face, the pink burning across the cheekbones as if still lit by the flames. Alice was pleased with herself even now, Emily realized, as the old woman popped a bread crust into her mouth. "How could you?" Emily said.

Theona flicked the tiny paper ball off her thumb, and it glanced off Alice's shoulder. "Fifty years is a long time to know somebody, but you can know somebody a whole lot longer and still not know what makes them be like they are," she said.

Alice nodded. "It's like I say, honey. Things always work out for the best. And if they don't," she shrugged and ate another bread crust, "well, life's too short to worry about it." She pushed herself up on her arms, leaned across the table and kissed Theona full on the mouth. Theona's pudgy hand came up around Alice's shoulder, and her chipped orange nails flickered against the pink tulips on Alice's dress.

In the instant of the women's embrace, someone entered the building from the Avenue de Ursulines, a deadbolt clicked open, a bag of garbage tipped in the stairwell. From behind a closed door, a woman shouted "Oh Christ Jesus, can't you please just leave me alone?" But Emily didn't move. With her chin propped on her fist, she studied the lines of the old bodies coming together, and the shadows between them fell to her place at the table.

The Mask

SUSAN HAD SEEN THE MASK BEFORE, but when Jeremy came downstairs wearing it that morning, he startled her. She'd been rummaging through the drawer for her sunglasses and turned around, quick, to tell him to hurry, to say he was almost late for school, and he stood there on the bottom step, grinning. Or, at least she'd imagined he was grinning. The mask made a terrible face, partway between a grimace and a leer, and when Susan jumped, she fumbled her glasses onto the floor, then said crossly, "Hurry up, you've got exactly seven minutes before school starts."

Jeremy pulled the mask up by the chin and his face, round and sunburned, was grinning. "Were you scared?" he said.

"Come on," she insisted. "Put on your shoes. Let's go."

He lifted the mask clear of his head and handed it over. "I'm taking this in for my sharing," he said, and Susan put it into his backpack without looking at it while he put on his shoes.

Once outside they hurried down the sidewalk. The school was a block away and they usually seemed to push their departure time to the limit, to leave six minutes, four minutes before the bell, so that mornings were languid and then ended in a sudden, last-minute rush. It was May, and warm, with a steady cool breeze bringing the scent of lilacs, heavy and sweet over the faint clean fragrance of the evergreens. Susan's husband joked that in a few years their yard would be a forest, that they'd need a map to find the front door. The first year they'd had the house, she asked for a tree on Mother's Day, and it had become the traditional gift. As she and Jeremy hurried on, they passed the crab apple, the hawthorne, the

125

shadblow, the small, fiery new Japanese maple moored to the earth with guy wires. Susan knew they'd eventually have to stop buying trees—their yard was only a medium-sized lot—but she didn't like to think about that time. The trees were permanent; they seemed almost a memorial to something, though she couldn't say what. She remembered vividly each trip to the nursery, each planting, moving the burlap-balled sapling around the yard until they found the right spot. They'd given her other gifts before they'd started giving trees, but now she didn't remember them.

They passed the Pattersons' stone Cape Cod, then waited for the traffic to clear at the corner. For a few weeks in the fall, Jeremy had wanted to walk to school alone. She'd crossed the street with him, then stood, watching him run to the white fence at the top of the hill. She always felt uneasy, not knowing if he went directly into school then, or if he dawdled on the hillside the way she'd seen other children do in the mornings. Eventually, he decided he'd rather have someone to talk to than independence, and she walked the whole way with him again, alert for a sign that he was humoring her.

They'd gone only a few steps on the other side of the street when Jeremy stopped and squatted beside an anthill rising from the crack between two squares of sidewalk. "Mom," he said. "It's like Teotihuacan!"

Susan glanced at her watch and then at the anthill, which lay like a handful of red earth on the gray concrete. A few small red ants wandered aimlessly, and Susan thought if there was a major project in the works for this colony, then clearly these ants weren't in on it.

"Teotihuacan?" she said, and touched the top of his head. "Let's go."

Jeremy stood and shouldered his backpack. His first grade class was studying Mexico, and as they walked he told Susan about the huge and beautiful Toltec city, about buildings surfaced in mosaic, about the artifacts in clay and stone that archaeologists still unearthed from its ruins.

126

"I'm going to say my mask is an artifact," he said, and stopped, unzipped the backpack and lifted out the mask. He'd made it a few years earlier, in a Saturday morning art class he'd eventually lost interest in. The teacher had spread gesso over translucent Halloween masks and told the class to decorate the white surface. Though Jeremy's mask had once been of a heavy-browed, frowning man, almost a parody of wretchedness and concern, he'd painted it tiger-lily orange, with vertical black lines on the cheeks, flashes of ultramarine around the nostrils, and glued feathery red tissue paper across the forehead. It was the face of a god, an idol, a jungle warrior from an extinct civilization. The black spines around the eye-holes shadowed her son's pale blue eyes as they darted from side to side, the only animated part of that fierce and fixed and primitive expression.

Susan reached out her hand. She wanted to tell Jeremy to take the mask off, to save it for his sharing time, but he was a-head of her now and the distance between them grew by the second. "Goodbye," he called, already running down the hill to where the children waited in orderly lines, their faces turned toward him like sunflowers obedient to the transit of sustaining light.

Guitar

Mary Craine

MARY CRAINE PENNIMAN heard the back door shut quietly, then her son appeared in the yard below. He pulled a blue watch cap down over his ears and looked up at the window. Mary Craine waved but Nate turned before she lowered her hand; he stuffed his hands into his coat pockets and walked into the woods as if he hadn't seen her, balancing his weight on his heels, moving so silently that if she let herself, she might almost think he was a breeze that sighed through the spaces between the trees. In her arms Abigail woke up, turned her head toward her mother's breast and began to nuzzle with faint mewings. Mary Craine fumbled at the buttons of her shirt, then guided the child's mouth over the nipple. Abigail began to suck and the breast tingled with the pull of the milk. Mary Craine wiped the window where her breath had fogged it. Nate was nowhere in sight. Sunlight fell thin and white through bare branches and pressed shadows on the path mounded with leaves his footsteps hadn't stirred.

She pulled the blanket close around Abigail's shoulder. This morning frost had blackened the last of the marigolds and at noon, the temperature was in the twenties. Last night when she and Jack met Nate at the Lake Charles airport, they said he'd brought the cold air with him. But Nate loved the cold; his first autumn in Philadelphia had given him buoyance, made him move a little faster, talk a little brisker than he had four months ago.

The floorboards creaked down the hall under Jack's boots. Mary Craine heard his feet on the soft carpet of the bedroom and in a few steps, he stood behind her at the window, his hand on her shoulder, his lips in her hair. He reached around her for Abigail, touched the baby's pink skin and smoothed with one finger the blonde fuzz on the baby's lopsided skull. "I still can't believe it," he said. Mary Craine let herself rest in the circle of his arm. He stroked up the side of Abigail's face and rested his fingers over his wife's breast, where the milk pulsed, then touched her other breast, damp in its cradle of flannel and leaking milk.

She was standing at the stove with a wooden spoon in her hand, stirring soup, when Nate returned to the house near dark. He stopped just inside the open door to take off his sneakers, and the cold air poured in around him.

"Would you close the door while you take those off?" Mary Craine said, pointing with the spoon.

"Spoon's dripping," he said, and slammed the door.

"Thanks."

He padded over to the stove and his hair swung forward across his cheek as he leaned to smell the soup.

Mary Craine tucked the hair behind his ear. "When do you plan to cut this mess?"

"Maybe never." He grinned and tasted the spoonful of soup she offered.

"I thought long hair was passé now, a relic."

"Guess again," he said. "The soup needs salt. And something else. Basil? Can you put basil in potato soup?"

"You can *do* anything . . . "

"That's the spirit, Ma," he said.

" . . . but I can't promise how it'll taste."

"Let's find out." He took a beer out of the refrigerator and sat down at the counter. "You want one?"

"I shouldn't. I'm nursing."

"You're kidding. You can't have a beer? One beer?"

"I don't want a drunk baby on my hands." She smiled. "Besides, I might want a glass of wine with dinner."

"That's cool." He drank slowly from the bottle, his eyes half-closed, one leg swinging as if in time with music playing in his head. Then he set the bottle down and said, "Why should I cut it? Dad's hair was long, past his shoulders, even."

"Everybody's hair was long back then."

"I'll bet his hair would still be long."

Mary Craine shook her head. "I don't think so. Nobody looks like they used to. Your dad wouldn't look the same either."

"Yeah?" Nate sounded skeptical.

"Well, look at me. Remember those old pictures?"

"Yeah," Nate said, "but you're different." Then he smiled. "Remember that one from *Blindness?*"

Mary Craine nodded, recalling the liner photograph on J.W.'s second album. Her hair fell nearly to her waist; it was straight, blond, and studded with flowers. She was pregnant with Nate then and J.W. always said the white gauze dress stretched across her belly made her look like Mother Nature on the margarine commercial.

She smiled. "It seems kind of silly now, doesn't it?"

"No," Nate said. "You were beautiful, Mom."

"Well, we were beautiful people," Mary Craine said, and pulled a wry face.

"I've decided I'm not going to cut my hair until summer," he said. "I want to see if I like it."

Jack came into the kitchen with Abigail asleep on his shoulder. "See if you like what?" he said.

"Long hair," Nate said. "I'm growing my hair."

"Yeah? I hadn't noticed," Jack said. He smiled and made as if to tousle Nate's hair but Nate pulled away. "My hair used to be long," Jack said. "I looked pretty scruffy for a while there, too." Jack's curly hair was gray now; Mary Craine thought sometimes the ringlets on his head made him look like a wise cherub. Only his moustache was still tipped with blond.

"I'll bet you were a real hippie," Nate said, taking another sip of the beer.

"I didn't say that, Nate. I just said my hair was long."

"Well, I'll bet that long hair did you a lot of good the whole time you were researching the Civil War. I mean, how relevant can you get?"

133

Jack smiled thinly. "There are parallels, if you want to pursue them," he said.

"Nate," Mary Craine said, "the table needs setting. Jack, would you put Abigail down so we can eat before she wakes up?"

But Jack was already heading for the living room. Mary Craine could tell he wanted to pursue the parallels; he had that expression, his classroom face as she thought of it. But she couldn't stand to hear them argue right now—Jack sure of himself, Nate in over his head but refusing to admit it.

Nate pulled open the silverware drawer, then closed it and went to the kitchen sink to wash. He lathered his hands, then soaped his face.

Mary Craine watched him, silencing the automatic plea that the kitchen sink was for dishwashing. His back to her, she noticed how his shoulders had broadened, how his torso tapered sharply to his hips. He would never be much taller than he was now, she knew that—he was at least four inches shorter than she was. J.W. had stood barely five-six, but he'd liked to show off her height. He bought her expensive leather boots with high heels, shawls, straight-leg blue jeans to cover her long legs. When they stood side-by-side, J.W. Sonnier had come up to her shoulder.

Nate reached for the dish towel. "Are you angry with me?" he said, wiping his face.

"A little."

"What's the problem?"

"What's your problem? Why are you picking at Jack this way? You've been at his throat since you got home."

In the living room Abigail began to cry and Jack shushed her, singing a song about a dead gray goose as he walked her around in front of the fire.

"Cute," Nate said. "You have to admit it. They're very cute together."

"Nate, don't be a smart-ass. She's your sister."

"Half-sister," he corrected.

"Okay." Mary Craine let out a deep breath. "But still your sister."

Nate seemed to consider this for a minute. Then he grinned. "Jesus, Ma. You know she could be my daughter? When she's my age I'll be thirty-six, same as you are now." Mary Craine turned back to the stove and soon heard him slamming down forks, knives and spoons on the wooden table.

Abigail stayed awake through dinner, staring blankly at the candle flames. Jack held her while Mary Craine ate, then Mary Craine took her. Abigail was no trouble; she was a quiet baby, just as Nate had been. Mary Craine tried to spread Abigail's fingers out, to uncurl them inside her own palm, but the baby's hands only gripped her finger more tightly. Abigail yawned, her large eyes closed and Mary Craine kissed the top of her head, breathing in the warm animal smell. She had forgotten this musk of blood and afterbirth that clung to the child during the first months; she had always remembered Nate as a new baby smelling of talcum powder and sweet soap.

Maybe I noticed less at eighteen, she thought; she put her cheek against Abigail's head and tried to summon back the feeling she'd had when Nate lay in her arms just this way. She remembered little; back then she thought Nate would be the first of many children she and J.W. would have. But by the time Nate was two, J.W. was dead.

Now she looked across the table at Nate and saw a man who looked the way J.W. Sonnier had at twenty, the year she married him. "Foxface" was the nickname she had given J.W., and in Nate, Mary Craine could see how accurate she had been. The pointed face, narrow at the chin and wide across the cheekbones, was surrounded by straight reddish-gold hair.

When Nate looked up at her, his eyes were small, hard points of blue. "More bread?" he asked, holding out the empty basket.

Nate finished his dinner quickly, cleared his dishes and went upstairs, mumbling "goodnight" though it was barely seven o'clock.

"What's with him?" Jack said.

"He's angry. Maybe about Abigail, I don't know," Mary Craine offered.

Jack shook his head. "That's a new one. The whole time you were pregnant he seemed excited. Now that the baby's here, he's jealous."

"It's just a guess. He hasn't said much."

Jack buttered a piece of bread. "Maybe it's something else, then. Has he said anything about his grades?"

"Nothing. I started to talk but he found some excuse to leave the house. He's spent more time in the woods today than he has in the house."

"Maybe he's having girl trouble."

"Nate?" Mary Craine shifted Abigail the way she liked to be held, face down across Mary Craine's lap. "He hasn't mentioned that he's seeing anyone."

Jack grinned. "Where is it written that a boy his age has to discuss his love life with his mother?"

"Nate always has."

They heard John Lee Hooker start up loud upstairs, then almost immediately Nate turned the volume down. In high school he had confiscated J.W.'s record collection, and Mary Craine was amused—these songs had been his lullabies. When Nate was a baby he could sleep at parties, concerts, recording sessions, waking only when the music stopped.

In that way, he was like J.W. For a while people said J.W. Sonnier was going to be the best white blues guitarist in the world. Mary Craine could still hear what they meant on the albums, that wailing like a man who knew he was doomed, a thin thread of sorrow cutting in over the steady pulse of the amplified heartbeat. She wasn't sure how J.W. had learned to play like that; she doubted J.W. even knew. He was a doctor's son from Beauville, Louisiana, and his family always thought his guitar playing was diversion, that hanging around black clubs in Opelousas and Vinton was something he'd give up once he got his life on track.

After J.W. died people came to this house to ask Mary Craine what he had been like; they wondered if she'd seen his death coming. Even as she held Nate on her lap and answered them politely, she could see their satisfaction in her ignorance, that after all she was just like they were—J.W. had fooled them all. The night he smashed his motorcycle into the back of a broken-down van in Big Sur, she was at this house outside Lake Charles with the baby and a nanny who called herself Sunshine. The next morning when J.W.'s manager phoned and said, "I've got some tough news," Mary Craine had sighed, steeling herself for another story of a mangled performance, of J.W. too stoned to get through the last set or not showing up at all.

Mary Craine looked around at the high white walls of the dining room, the arched windows of uneven glass that had been here for a century. As soon as there was money, J.W. bought the house for her, and it was paid for when he died, but he had lived in it only a few days a month, for a few years. It wasn't posh, like the big houses some of his friends owned; it was Victorian, built by a lumber baron in the only boom this region had ever known and sold in the thirties, when all the trees left were those growing in the patch of woods between this house and the creek. Now she carried her sleeping baby to the window and looked out at the night. On one side of the house were soybean fields, on the other, woods, but now she couldn't tell the difference. She rocked from side to side almost unconsciously, lulling Abigail with her body, as she had before the child's birth. In the rippled window the movement was ghostlike, blurred and wavering, and after a while she turned away.

After she laid Abigail in her crib, Mary Craine climbed the stairs and knocked on Nate's door. In high school he had taken his things from the big rear bedroom on the second floor, where Abigail now slept, and moved them to the small empty room on the third. He'd painted the walls and floor deep, vibrating magenta. Being inside the room made Mary

Craine think of standing inside a large bruised mouth. She hesitated, then knocked again.

"It's open," he called.

He lay on his narrow brass bed, a blanket half-covering his legs. He'd taken off his shoes, but he still wore his jeans and sweater, and his face was puffy, as if he had been sleeping. J.W.'s *Blindness* album played softly on the stereo.

"Are you okay?" Mary Craine sat down beside him and touched his forehead. His skin was cool.

"Sure."

"Been sleeping?"

"Halfway," he said. "Just listening to music."

She picked up the scuffed album jacket. J.W.'s face glistened in the red light, and around his forehead a leather band held his bright hair out of his eyes, held it straight as it spilled down across his shoulders. His thin fingers blurred over the strings of his guitar and his eyes were closed. With his head held back like that, he looked like a man oblivious to everything but the sound he was making, a man who couldn't answer if you called him. She put the album jacket on the bed.

"I always liked this album," she said.

"Yeah," Nate said. He raised himself up on his elbows. "It's like you can hear everything he ever felt about himself in that guitar. Listen to this riff." He leaned over and turned up the volume. Mary Craine thought about Abigail sleeping below them, and almost asked him to turn it down. But she listened, head bent, until the song was over.

"Nobody's played like that since," Nate said.

"He was good."

"Good?" Nate laughed. "Jesus, he was terrific. There's nobody like him."

"I guess not."

"The whole thing's bizarre to me," he said. "It's like, when the kids at school find out he's my father, they freak."

Mary Craine smoothed the long hair back from his forehead. "I wouldn't get too caught up in all that, if I were you."

"Why not?"

138

"It has so little to do with you, Nate."

"What do you mean? He's my father, isn't he?"

"But his life was one thing; our life now is something different. He had more bad times than good, believe me."

"Oh sure," Nate said. "Playing with the Stones really must have been shitty. And he must've hated doing that Filmore concert with Joplin."

"It wasn't that great," Mary Craine said. "The Filmore concert wasn't even recorded. He played back-up lead on three tracks on the Stones album. What does that add up to? Fifteen minutes?"

"But it's a terrific fifteen minutes. And there were his own albums."

"Three albums, Nate." Mary Craine shook her head. "An hour-and-a-half of music. Less than the time it took you to get home yesterday."

"Don't hand me that, Ma. Ten times that—twenty times that—went into every song he wrote. And then the time he spent practicing—he worked years to do those albums. He was a whole lifetime getting to those songs. Who cares how many there are?"

"I'm not saying he didn't work hard for what happened to him."

"Then what are you saying?"

"That it was hard for me, and it would've been hard for you if you'd been anything but a baby then. J.W. never was easy to live with. He mostly just wasn't *there*, you know, even when he was sitting right in front of you."

"You're making Dad out to be some kind of monster," Nate said. "Like Jack Penniman came along and rescued you from the big bad wolf."

"Jack didn't rescue me from anybody," Mary Craine said. "I did just fine on my own for ten years."

"I was there, remember?"

"The music isn't everything, Nate. Don't think it can be."

He sat up. "Listen," he said, "what I want to know is isn't he still there for you? I mean, don't you think about

139

him at all anymore? Or do you just sort of pretend he never happened? Maybe you think I came from the fairies or something?"

"I can't live my whole life as J.W. Sonnier's widow. Is that what you want?"

"I don't want anything. I'm a big boy now. You do what you want."

"I'm trying to."

"Time for something else now, huh?"

"That's right."

"Time to play mama again."

"Something like that." Mary Craine touched Nate's arm. "That's what's bothering you?"

He yawned and dropped back onto the pillow. "School's tough, Ma. Jack's right—Penn isn't high school."

"Are you doing okay?"

"I won't flunk out. Maybe I'll decide on a major one of these days."

"I didn't mean that," she said. "I mean, are you really okay? Are you okay inside?"

" 'Got a lot on my mind, got a girl on the line . . . ' ' he laughed, singing the lyrics to one of J.W.'s songs. "Hey, was that girl you, Ma?"

Mary Craine stood up. "No," she said. "It wasn't. Not that time."

She heard the steady hum the dishwasher made, and when she went to the kitchen she found Jack standing beside the counter, waiting for the coffee to brew. He was reading, underlining passages with a chewed pencil in a book open flat on the countertop. She brushed past him to get the coffee mugs. The cabinets were high, with shelves to the ceiling, and the milky blue ceramic mugs she wanted—the ones she bought years ago in Nebraska when J.W. did a concert there—were on the top shelf. She liked the pearly glaze, the rounded contours; tonight she felt a particular desire to use them again.

Jack looked up from his book and smiled. "All quiet upstairs?" he said.

140

"Abigail's asleep. Nate's listening to music. I don't know if you can call it quiet."

"Did you talk?"

"A little." Mary Craine set the mugs on the counter and poured in the coffee. "He's been thinking about J.W."

"J.W.?" Jack closed his book, using the pencil as a bookmark.

She shrugged. "Nate wants to know him." She took the carton of milk from the refrigerator and poured a dollop in each cup. The coffee swirled with lighter color as she stirred it. "Nobody could explain J.W.," she said. "All Nate hears is that guitar. He thinks that's all there was to it."

"How's he supposed to know anything different?" Jack said.

"What would you have me tell him?" she said. "I try to think about the good things. I remember how funny J.W. could be sometimes. How smart he was. I tell Nate how much J.W. loved him, how J.W. used to hold him sometimes and you could see he was just about to bust open from loving him so much."

Jack picked up his mug and drank off a little of the coffee. "Do you think you're being fair?"

"Fair?"

"Fair," he said. His face was open and pleasant, as if, Mary Craine thought, he were debating with one of his students. He smiled. "It would be easy for Nate to idolize J.W., don't you think?"

"Jack, one of the first things he wanted when he got home last night was J.W.'s album of press clippings. According to that, his father was the next best thing to Jesus Christ."

"That's exactly my point," Jack said. "Don't you think you have some responsibility to balance the picture now that Nate's an adult?"

"Why now?"

Jack shrugged. "I'm not sure that too much J.W. would be good for him. Nate deserves to have his own life."

She picked up her coffee cup, warming her hands on the

sides. "You act like he's supposed to forget where he came from."

"Did I say that?"

"That's what you meant. You wish him well, I know." She sipped her coffee. "But Nate hears J.W.'s music. He feels it. He knows what's going on inside." She wished she could explain to Jack why she had loved J.W. She put down her cup and touched his wrist. "Jack?" she said.

He smiled at her. "What?"

She squeezed his hand. His brown eyes looked at her warmly. "You look tired," she said. "You get to bed early tonight, you hear?"

Nate

Nate heard his mother talking to his stepfather downstairs, and imagined the two of them drinking coffee at the kitchen table, their heads bent earnestly together. He imagined his mother's face, lined and still beautiful in the warm light, her eyes light blue and flecked with gold, her wide mouth forming a kiss as she sipped the hot coffee. She lifted one thin hand to her hair, pushed it back over her shoulder, and the hair fell like fabric down her back. In the lamplight the gold ring on her hand shone; perhaps she placed her hand at the neck of her dark sweater, or over her breasts as she sometimes did now, unconsciously, as if they called for her attention. Sometimes when she lifted her sweater to feed the baby Nate found himself staring; her breasts, which had always been small, were full now, and Abigail's greedy pink mouth sucked noisily at them. He tried to remember himself as a boy burrowing into his mother's bony chest, and her hand stroking back his hair. He tried to recall her thin arms, her sweet, faintly lemony smell. Her smell was different now.

Nate thought about his stepfather's face: grim if they were talking about him, the worry line between the shaggy brows and the mouth under the thick moustache turned down heavily at the corners. Sometimes Jack stroked the ends of

142

the moustache with his thumb and forefinger when he listened to someone speak; when Nate was younger he would mimic this movement in the mirror. He accepted that Jack Penniman was kind but a creature of many laughable habits that came from living a long time alone. Jack was thirty-four when he married the boy's mother, his only marriage, though he spoke occasionally of other women he had known; Nate thought this was in bad taste and tried never to appear interested in what Jack said about them. Jack taught American history at McNeese and encouraged the boy to go away to school, though most of Nate's high school friends went to state schools and Jack himself graduated with honors from L.S.U. "I didn't have a trust fund to get me into the Ivy League," Jack said when the acceptance came from Penn. Nate was pleased to be going to a good school, but guessed that his stepfather really wanted him out of the house. Last night, coming in from his midnight walk in the woods, he passed their bedroom door and heard his mother's breath coming short and hard. He paused, then stomped up the stairs, almost hoping to wake the baby.

Alone now in his room, Nate thought of the girl he made love to this fall, Anna Paz, a state senator's daughter from New Jersey. He liked the way Anna was easy about sex; it was no big deal, even the first time when he was nervous as hell. She said she'd slept with many other guys who were nervous and at first he thought this should bother him, but now it didn't, seeming simply part of her direct way. She was different from his high school girlfriend, whose caresses had been laced with restrictions and payoffs; he knew when Anna wanted him. She was plump and dark; she preferred black high heels and hats with netting draped over her eyes; she believed in telling the truth even when it hurt his feelings. Often she shook him by the shoulders and said in her mock-tough voice, "Tell me what you're thinking even if it's something bad." Often he found himself on the brink of saying *you make too much noise, you shouldn't eat that donut, your hair needs washing* but always, he was checked by

143

politeness. Anna dreamed of becoming a famous fabric designer like Marimekko; when they lay together on her bed in the disorderly apartment she shared with four other girls, she spoke about these dreams and he wanted to say *You will never be famous, your designs aren't that good,* but he stopped himself. He wanted her to go on being cheerful and knew the truth would only depress her, and she would cry the way she did when she spoke of her mother's lover who stayed at her parents' house when the legislature was in session. Away from Anna, Nate thought there was at least a kind of beauty in the overlapping design her mouth made in the small wet circles across his stomach, and he shouldn't mind that she would never be famous for geometric shapes on a bolt of cloth. He liked to walk everywhere with her in the gray cold afternoons when they should have been studying. They walked on campus and in town, on Chestnut, Locust, Walnut, Juniper—streets bright with restaurants and bookstores and markets, where he was one face in a stream of faces, remarkable only for his shock of bright hair and the girl in dramatic clothes who walked beside him.

Nate swung his legs off the bed, took his jacket from the chair and clattered down three flights of stairs. In the kitchen his mother looked up from her coffee and Jack looked up from his book, pencil poised.

"Out," Nate said when his mother asked where he was going.

Jack

When the door slams I'm looking at her, and she jumps like she's been slapped, and starts upstairs though the baby hasn't cried out. In a few minutes she's back in the kitchen, rubbing her arms.

"I thought I heard Abigail." She looks out the glass of the back door as if she expects to see where he's gone but of course she can't see anything but herself; outside is dark and inside she has the light on over the table. She puts her hands on either side of the door frame and for a minute I think she might shake it or start to cry, but she's only stretching her arms over her head, popping the kinks from her spine. She has on red high-top sneakers, jeans that sag in the ass, a pilled blue sweater that used to be yours. She drops her hands to her hips and sways from side to side.

"Tired?"

"Yeah." She does a few knee bends, all the time watching her reflection in the glass.

I look back at the book I'm reading, at the passages underlined in black. It's late and my eyes burn. I wonder why the type in the book is so small and the photographs so large. I wonder if my students even read the text or if they page through the book, looking with mild, blank eyes at the photographs before going on to the summary enclosed in a red box on the final page of each chapter.

"Did you hear me?" she says.

"What?"

"I said, I don't think it's such a great idea for him to be wandering around out there alone at night."

I close the book again. "Why?"

"Suppose he steps on a snake?" She turns away from the door, sits back down at the table and lifts her cup. "That happened to somebody I knew. This guy in J.W.'s band. Lonnie was in the woods hunting with his brother and he stepped on a cottonmouth. It killed him." She sets the cup down. "Did you make enough coffee for me to have another cup?"

"Sure." I pour out more coffee for both of us and sit down next to her at the table. "Listen," I touch her hair, smooth it down over her shoulder. "Don't worry about Nate. He'll be fine. Snakes don't lie around on paths at night. It's too cold. They curl up under rocks."

"How do you know Nate stays on the path?" she says. She fidgets away from my hand. "Why does he go out there anyway?"

"Restless. Didn't you do things like that when you were his age?"

She shrugs. "When I was his age he was a baby. I couldn't leave a tiny baby to go walking around in the dark in the woods."

"Didn't you want to sometimes?"

"Oh," she says. "Sure. Who wouldn't. But, well—you know." She shrugs again.

I look at her and smile, and try to think of something positive to say. I've been married to this woman for six years and I'm still uncomfortable with the way silences rear up between us when all I want is an ordinary time. When I read she sits and stares into space intently, as if she's listening for something. When I talk she listens and nods, but it's the way she might respond to a prattling child. Now she touches my hand and smiles back at me, and I feel like Abigail, like Nate, like I used to feel when my mother would pat my hand and tell me that someday I was going to be brilliant, she knew it, now get outside and play. What would you have done at Mary Craine's touch? Laughed? Slapped her hand away?

The first time I saw Mary Craine was at a party and she was there with Mike, one of my grad students who got drunk an hour into the party and collapsed on a bench in the courtyard with his drunk cronies. Mike was an old friend, she said when I started talking to her on the couch, somebody she'd known for years. She smiled and said that his getting drunk didn't matter to her, he could find his way home all right. She wore a blue dress that looked like a long T-shirt and she was barefoot. She crossed her legs and as I talked she swung her top leg in time to the music on the stereo. I thought she wasn't listening; I thought she was off somewhere in the music, putting up with my conversation. I figured I'd give her an easy out; I offered to get her another beer. When I came back, she was still sitting there, swinging her leg, drumming her fingers on the sofa arm. "Listen," she said. "After we finish this beer, could you take me home? I came in Mike's car and I don't want him to drive me, drunk as he is. And I promised my son I'd be home before eleven." She talked about her son; he was twelve, she said. I had a hard time believing she had a child at all, especially one almost a teenager. When I said this, she laughed. "I'm already thirty," she said, and I liked that about her: she wasn't coy about her age as some women might be. When she got up from the couch I saw that she was exactly my height: six feet. That bothered me a little; I'd never been with a woman that tall. She looked around on the floor for a minute to find her sandals and then we left without saying goodbye to anybody. On the drive to her house I was nervous; I didn't know what she wanted, if she'd invite me in and if she did, if that meant she wanted to make love. But in the car she seemed not to regard me as a man, as a sexual being—she spoke to me as casually as if she expected me to be there, as if I'd always been there. Did she do this with you, the first time you saw her at the Royal Cafe, and bought her a Coke, and talked to her while the other patrons laughed at your long hair?

The first time out to the house, the road seemed rougher than it ever did again; she hadn't mentioned how far away she lived and I had a silly moment of panic when I wondered if I was being set up for something, if she had a gun, if she was crazy and wanted my car. When I drove up the gravel driveway I had another surprise. The house was a restored Victorian, white clapboard and green shingles, gingerbread trim. The porch light was on. I hadn't expected this: usually when people live out in the country around here, it's a cheap farmhouse they've gotten a deal on. We talked for a while with the engine running, then she said she'd better get inside. She hesitated, then invited me in for coffee.

Nate was still up, lying on the floor in the living room reading. He looked at me as if he wanted me to drop dead, but was polite enough finally. He was already a smart kid, and good-looking in a scruffy, teenaged way. When he saw that I was only having coffee in the kitchen, he kissed his mother goodnight and went upstairs. But he turned his stereo on loud so I wouldn't forget about him. I was still nervous but Mary Craine seemed not to notice; in her vague, distracted way she was kinder to me than any woman had ever been. When we finally did make love at my apartment nearly a month later, I said truthfully that I loved her and she smiled, silent, and touched my forehead as if searching for a fever.

By then, of course, she'd told me about you. I was surprised at first, as anyone would be. I'd listened to your music a bit in college, so she didn't have to explain who you were when she told me your name. Even in college you were not one of my favorites, though I knew you were good—the music always struck me as being a little too raw. On nights when I went out drinking with friends, I always liked the songs but they made me uncomfortable, always probing into the same emotions I felt were best downplayed. It's only a matter of taste; just as I don't understand men who say they'd love to have spent one night with Janis Joplin, I was never the sort to lean my head back and grin or break into sentimental tears when you ran your fingers over the strings of your guitar, though I've seen plenty of people do it.

I don't listen to your records now, of course, but if I did I'm not sure I could hear the music in the same way. I'd end up listening for a clue in the sound that would tell me why Mary Craine loved you, why she put up with your drinking, the drugs, the women you slept with on the road and then taunted her about when you came home. She is still a beautiful woman but at twenty, her face had the freshness that most women don't hold onto very long; looking at pictures of her then, I see a softness about her face that wasn't there when I met her ten years later and isn't there now. Sometimes when I look into her face, which is lined and thinner now, I'm angry that it was you who had her when she was at her peak, and you didn't care, didn't appreciate her beauty. When she hands me a cup of coffee and a plate of something she's baked I look at her hands and remember that she crushed a lit cigarette out on your cheekbone one afternoon when she came home and found you making love to a local groupie on the living room sofa. When she was in labor for twelve hours with Abigail, I kept thinking about what she'd told me of her longer labor with Nate, when you dropped acid after two hours and took off into the woods because you said you couldn't stand her suffering, and her parents had to take her to the hospital. Last night when, after waiting the prescribed three weeks, I made love to Mary Craine the first time since Abigail's birth, and when she was asleep beside me, I thought about what she'd told me of another time: when the week-old Nate lay sleeping in the bassinet beside the bed, and you wanted sex though she cried out when you entered her and, enduring you, she bit her lips until they bled.

Though I had lovers when I was single, I always played by the rules: I never slept with students, had affairs with married women, picked up women in bars. Until I met Mary Craine I had never dated a woman with a child. My lovers were usually my colleagues in other departments. They were intelligent and good-looking women in their thirties who liked to be alone to do their own work, who wore crisp tailored jackets and silk blouses with their plaid skirts, dark cotton instead of wool but still an affectation of the Eastern schools. They were brisk, efficient women, good teachers of good classes—women who managed to be both passionate and careful in bed, exercising their great control even over sex, that last seemingly ungovernable frontier. And they were completely unsympathetic when I gave up their good company for Mary Craine's—a woman who is not brisk but has the confidence of those sure of their own historical importance, who half the time dresses like a boy, who left school at sixteen to marry an unemployed guitarist—a woman who told me once, in our first year of marriage when I still believed she needed intellectual interests, that she thought Randy Newman's *Good Old Boys* album was more profound than *The Waste Land*.

Shortly before we married I was buttonholed after a committee meeting by an assistant professor of political science, a woman with whom I had a brief, chaotic affair a year or two earlier. "Jack," she said, already laughing at the joke she'd prepared, "is it really true you're going to marry Big Bird?"

For possibly the first time in my life, I was speechless. Almost instinctively I pulled a cigarette from my jacket pocket and knocked it against my wrist, tamping the tobacco down too hard to get a good draw. I looked into the woman's up-turned face, stalling. She stood close to me with her teeth bared in a wide smile that showed her gums, one hand pulling at my arm in what so many women think is an affectionate gesture. Her short black hair was streaked with gray. Grooves in her forehead showed the way she arched her thin brows for emphasis, making her point in the classroom or in bed, I'd seen the same gesture both places. Under the husky, laughing patter she began to cover my failure to reply, I heard something else, a kind of hysteria that spoke of her own failure to figure out why I wanted someone obviously less well educated, less intelligent than she. And I saw, standing in the air-conditioned committee room, with my colleagues clustered in groups around me, talking with earnest faces about procedural violations in the standing committees, what my life before Mary Craine was destined to be: to marry this woman who stood before me or someone much like her, engage in intelligent conversation, conduct adequate research in our separate fields—a seamless life lived between class and the committee room, departmental party and the sack. And I saw, too, as the woman backed away, still smiling, pleased that she'd scored her intended victory but a little confused that I hadn't at least put up a fight, that what I wanted from Mary Craine was release from the bitterness of women who'd suf-fered at the hands of men they didn't love, or didn't love more than they loved themselves. I wanted to be loved like she had loved you. I wanted to be with a woman who was capable of loving like that. I left the committee meeting, drove out to her house and sat down for supper at her table. She spoke to me warmly, she laughed at a tired joke Nate told, she sat by herself on the porch while Nate and I cleaned up the dishes and talked about the Saints' problems at defense. And when I went out to her half an hour later, she was on the porch swing, the chains creaking as she pushed herself back and forth. When I stopped the swing to kiss her, I saw her eyes were wet. She looked up fiercely, as if she dared me to speak, but even in her fierceness, her look wasn't unkind. In her eyes at that moment—on the dim porch, with the smell of dying honeysuckle in the humid air—I saw that narrow margin between being lost and being saved; I was just learning it, but it was something she had already lived. It was something you'd taught her—maybe the only real thing of value you left her. I sat beside her on the swing and she pushed off again, her big bare feet whispering on the wooden porch.

Now I leave her with her coffee at the table and go up alone to the front bedroom, and turn back the quilt she made for the bed. She will wait at the table until Nate comes in, no matter how late. He walks to get away from me, to keep from having to see me with his mother, to keep from having to see Abigail, who proves to him that his mother and I love each other and have a life apart from him. I know he would trade me for you any day, though all he knows about you is your music. He thinks that's enough. But if I died tomorrow and left Abigail a few articles about Second Manassas as a way into my soul, wouldn't it be the same? If Mary Craine would permit it, I would take the boy into the woods and tell him about the man who fathered him, the man he should remember only because of a drunken spilling of seed into a seventeen-year-old girl on a tour bus going from city to city. I would tell him what he needs to know: that he can't measure passion by abstractions, by sound or color or even words. I would tell him the only redemption that lies ahead of him is in his own kindness, his own good deeds, his own work whenever he finds it. And I would say that if he finds himself bound to you, then he himself has forged the chain, because you had no interest in him either before his birth or afterwards, and told his mother as much, though she would never tell him. And you were certain of that, too, in your arrogance. In leaving them you became immortal; had you stayed Nate would have understood what you were: a low thing, full of cowardice, making only for yourself a music that others would take to be their own.

I turn off the light, and when I have lain awake long enough I get up and go into my daughter's room to be sure she is there, that she's still breathing. I lean over her crib, performing the ritual I am allowed now, in my fortieth year—that of a father kissing his child goodnight. She lies on her stomach, fists raised on either side of her head. My hand on her blanketed back rises and falls with her breathing.

Nate

It's cold, Anna, not the kind of cold you're used to but I'm freezing all the same. People around here say a wet cold feels colder. That first morning when we walked to class you wondered where all the birds were flying when they passed overhead in formation, a squadron heading south. They're here. My mother has feeders around the yard so sometimes when there's nothing better to do I watch the birds lining up at the troughs. At night they sleep in the woods, maybe in nests they built or maybe in nests some other birds left when they split for Cancun. I can hear them. I practice walking on the sides of my feet so I don't make noise but they know I'm here anyway and call out to each other down the path. I think about saving them the trouble, shouting out "Okay bird-brains, here I come," but I don't. Because maybe some crazy person really does hang out in the woods at night like my mother thinks. I don't take chances. Or, not that kind of a chance. Tonight before I came out here I listened five or six times to a song my father wrote called "Blue Goose" that had nothing to do with birds but was all about taking chances. There are no words, just my father's guitar, Lonnie on piano and Elliot on drums. In the music, every time my old man wades out into the water, you can hear the other two asking him to come back, but he says no, no, you two just got to follow. And the weird thing is, they do. And he keeps going farther, farther, until he's out so far you think he'll never come back. And you can feel why he doesn't want to: it's like he's suspended in another element, he's weightless, he has perfect control. And just then, right when you're not expecting anything but to keep on gliding through the water, he does this

152

incredible thing: he takes off and flies. And there's no way the other two can match that flight; they just tread water below him and watch as he does something they can never do, that they aren't even made for.

I never told you this, Anna (won't tell you now because I won't write this down, won't put any letter to you on paper to be left lying around in your parents' beige-on-beige palace in Passaic County), but sometimes the only place I want to get to is memory. Sometimes when I walk out here and it's still enough, dark enough, I feel as if I'm walking back to some place where I will know my father, as if I'm walking back through the sixteen years between today and the last time I saw him. I want my own memory of him, not something I've read or something my mother's told me.

Tonight I've walked all the way back to my earliest memory, of waking up in my mother's white iron bed in a room filled with sunlight. I look about two years old. My pajamas are the kind of cotton that has little dimples everywhere in the fabric, and they're printed with clowns juggling alphabet blocks. But when I wake up I realize gradually that I've wet the bed, that my pajamas and the white sheets are soaked and that all over I have the sticky, clammy feeling that comes from sleeping without air conditioning in summer. And then even more gradually, I realize that my mother is in the room. She's standing beside the bed in her yellow nightgown and her hair is loose, spilling like a robe across her bare arms. I reach up for her to hold me but she doesn't seem to see. She's talking on the telephone, and crying, and rasping out a sound like whea-ah, whea-ah, whea-ah, that I can still hear now if I try hard enough, and I know then, long before she ever tells me, that this sound she makes has something to do with my father. I start to cry really hard, and she picks me up, but still like she doesn't notice me, and presses me to her hip. Beyond this, I don't know if I'm remembering what happened, or if I'm piecing together what she told me later, or if this is only how I want it to be. But I can feel my wet clothes making her nightgown wet, and I clamp my legs around her waist. I put my head on her chest and can feel where the sound comes from and I think for a little while that it has nothing to do with my father, that the sound has been there all along inside her. I huddle close, sucking my thumb, waiting for the call to be over.

And it's this memory, Anna, that tells me I'll never be closer to my father than I am now. I keep going back, trying to force myself beyond that phone call, and it's like a window I can't break through. I can smell my mother's sweat, remember the texture of the skin of her neck, even know that the cry she made was in grief and in something like relief, like the sound hurt her when it was buried inside her as much as when it finally began to come out.

I know that on the other side of the glass my father waits for me. He was with me two years and all I have of that time are shadows, what people tell me happened. When I look in the mirror his face looks back at me. I listen to his music and I know what he was thinking as each finger slides over the strings. I walk in these woods, where my mother says he walked on nights when he wasn't ready to sleep, where he walked, she says, the night I was born. I walk until the path disappears and I'm walking through brush, breaking down scrub that wasn't here when my father walked here. I keep thinking that if I walk far enough he'll still be out here, I'll find him standing at the edge of the creek some night, his clothes muddy from the long walk, his face tired from the strain of waiting for me to come to him. But in the next second I know that it's only me who stands behind on the creek bank, marveling.

Mary Craine

A dark kitchen at night is a kind of closed workshop, the machinery cleaned and quiet, supplies lined up on the shelves, knives in the knife block, mallets and beaters hooked safely onto a pegboard. Nate's favorite book when he was small was about a kitchen at night that wasn't quiet at all, but a city of jam pots and salt boxes and oatmeal canisters where little boys got mixed into cake batter, slid into the oven to bake and came out smiling, wearing cake crust pajamas. I think a mother would never have written that book; she would have been too frightened, as I was, by the vision of her own child cooked up in a sticky covering, like napalm that coated the bodies of children in photographs we were beginning to see then, near the end of the war.

The digital clock on the microwave flashes 11:45 in green numbers. The floodlights carve white circles around the house and I imagine that in the dark outside the circles, our son who used to laugh at the boy getting baked in the cake is safe in the natural world, that he is in less danger there than in the streets of many cities, including the one where he now lives.

It wasn't until I had your child that I began to fear. For myself, I had no terror beyond the terror of the moment: I see myself at sixteen, swinging bare-headed and barefoot onto the back of your Harley, making the trip down a rutted dirt road to the field alongside the Sabine River, where we were married among a circle of friends. Our parents stayed away. We got so stoned that our friend who owned the field fell into the river and almost drowned. And a day or two later, we drove the Harley to New Orleans and stayed with people you knew there, or people we met—sleeping on a mattress in a walk-in closet, sleeping on the floor of the host's studio while the host got laid, sleeping on a sagging couch in somebody's kitchen. We bummed off your friends for weeks before we saved enough money from your gigs to get our own place. I was never afraid, not even the night at the Warehouse when I went for a soda and you thought I'd gone home with somebody else. I waited where we'd been sitting, but the people around there said you'd gone. When the concert was over and the mescaline I'd washed down had kicked in, I wandered alone beside the closed warehouses on Tchoupitoulas for over an hour, trying to remember where we lived, before I ran into somebody I'd met at one of the parties you took me to. He walked me to Fun's, bought me chili and coffee, and tried to call you. At four we gave up, walked back to his house and drank coffee until the buses started running at six and I could go home. Sitting in the safety of that hot city bus loaded with sleepy black women in starched white uniforms, on their way to clean houses and cook breakfasts, and listening to the low hum of their voices, I still didn't think about what might have happened. I closed my eyes against the sun already beating through the tinted glass, listened to the women's voices and didn't mind that my mouth felt like it had been coated with school paste and my clothes were clammy and wrinkled, that I smelled like sweat and greasy food and marijuana. I never saw the man again, but sometimes I wonder if he ever knew what happened to you, if he ever listened to the music and thought about that night. Or maybe he's forgotten it, the way you used to forget crazy things that sometimes happened to you.

When you were gone to L.A. or Chicago or wherever you were playing, Nate and I would stay at the house and I'd work on it, fixing the floors and painting, I did it all, remember that. And you'd call home every night, but after Nate was born something had changed. I knew how easy it was to make a life, what an accident it is that we're here at all. And then I figured if being here was that easy, it had to be just as easy to die. I had dreams sometimes, long before you died, that it was Nate I'd lose: I'd open the door to his room and find myself looking at nothing. I started to wonder how anyone ever found the strength to live after they lost somebody. You wanted me to come with you, leave Nate with Sunshine, but I couldn't do it. You were so ingrained in me I didn't even need to be with you to feel you were there; I tried to talk about this once but you said you couldn't listen anymore. All the partying that we'd started out doing together was over for me, but it was as if you couldn't stop, you just went at it harder once you were alone.

When Glen called that morning about the accident I'd been awake since before dawn. Nate woke up in the night and I took him into bed with me. I'd been lying beside him thinking about you, wondering if I'd really lost you for good this time. On your last trip home you'd said you found somebody you wanted to live with in California. I was rubbing Nate's back, looking at his fat legs and arms thrown out against the sheet and feeling scared for what his life would be like. And then I felt scared for my own life. I didn't want to go back to being just Mary Craine LeBlanc from Beauville, Louisiana, but I'd made the choice, hadn't I, in staying here? All those times you made the call, you wanted me with you. But this time when the phone rang and Glen was on the other end, I knew the choices didn't exist anymore.

When Nate began to grow up, I found Jack, all the time fearing it was already too late for me and Nate to start over with somebody else. You'd been with me half my life, though when I look back now I see that our marriage was short, just four years—already my marriage to Jack has lasted longer. Jack was so different from you I thought, I can put J.W. behind me now, have somebody that loves *me*. But when we knew Nate would be leaving for school I felt scared of being alone again, like Nate was still the only thing that existed of my real life. I had acted like Jack wasn't with me, that his coming home to me every night for five years had been nothing. And I knew that wasn't right. Maybe having another child was the only way I could get rid of you, get rid of that part of you that was still beating like a pulse. Abigail would be free of you, she'd be mine and Jack's, and grow up never needing to know you.

I held to that like a promise, all through the months Abigail was inside me, even these weeks since her birth. But when Nate came in from the woods before supper tonight, looking like you, asking about you, wanting you so badly, I saw that I was like that little boy in Nate's old storybook, who falls through the milk bottle and loses his cake covering.

Abigail cries out and I bring her downstairs to feed. We settle into the rocker beside the back door, where the light from the yard comes through, and I unwrap the tight blanket she likes to sleep in. In this dimness she opens her eyes and stares up at me as she nurses. At first she looked like a tiny, bald version of Jack, but now I can see something of myself in her

157

face, too, and something of my dead mother's face. I stroke Abigail's cheek and think how lucky she is not to know the cost of having this history, how lucky she is to lie in my arms and be warm, to feel the warm milk settle in her warm belly.

I sing to her, at first a song about a rambling man that you taught me, and when I finish that I sing everything I can remember to make her sleep again. She's so young that even her smiles are meaningless, though she smiles at me and I smile back. I carry her to the door and when I look out of the glass I see Nate coming into the circles the yardlights make in the darkness. As if he could hear me, I sing to him too, the syllables of your blues.

Migrations

MOTHER, YOU CAN'T KNOW how we hungered for the light. As we stood together on the shoreline this morning, we heard again and again the *lumaa, lumaa* the whale made in her grief, a close and resonant mourning. It was dawn we waited for, the twilight around noon that lifts the blank darkness over the flat land; we waited, too, for the icebreaker that carved islands of water from the white ice of the frozen ocean.

In the common room last night we listened late to the bellowing of the trapped whales, sat watching the ice and talking about them, all of us believing they would both be smothered by morning. The two grays, a mother and calf shoaled in by the ice for over a week, were already late for the journey south. Last night their bellowing had become all but intolerable, resonating off the ice, when one of the men began to tell a story from Kotzebue Sound, where in the trading post, he saw a boy of twelve or thirteen nursing from his mother. Someone else spoke up, said it's common among the Inuit there, a woman nursing her last child until it's nearly grown, nursing all her boys for as long as they want, some of them until they marry.

Most of the men laughed when he said this, but they were embarrassed, too, and Karin said they were evil-minded, that nothing but pure maternal love motivated the primitives. Then Vin, who has three little boys and a wife in Kenai, said there was no such thing as pure maternal love—that after Karin had seen a grown man nursing then she could talk to him about purity.

And then he started telling an Inuit story that I knew also, one we'd heard from old Aisa, of the blind boy who provided for his mother though she tricked him, told him that instead

161

of caribou he's killed his dog instead. As in most Inuit stories there's no reason given for her cruelty; up here I've noticed it's kindness that gets the explanation.

Vin leaned back in his chair, smoking. "The mother left him behind in the old snowhouse while she went to live with some other tribe. Pretty soon the kid gets hungry, you see. He has no place to go, to his own tribe he's a burden. So he calls out to a loon he hears overhead, and the loon comes, and because the boy doesn't kill it, it gives him back his sight. Now the boy can hunt game again. His mother, living on the fringe with another tribe, hears about his cure, comes back. She likes him again, likes the groceries. Then later, maybe years later, maybe it's days, I forget, one day he's out hunting whales. He ties his harpoon line around his mother's waist to brace himself. But as he throws the harpoon he lets go of the line, and the mother is dragged into the ocean. She's anchored into the back of a whale. And when she comes up for air, like the whales do, the boy on the ice says 'My mother is a fish's tail.' And the mother's out there hollering, 'Have pity on this poor woman, *lumaa, lumaa.*'"

"What's *lumaa?*" Karin wanted to know, fanning away Vin's cigarette smoke, looking annoyed.

"It means 'my son did it,'" he said, and grinned. "One word for what it takes us a whole sentence to say. Sometimes the Inuit say *lumaa* is what the whales sing, it's the song she taught them."

And Mother, that's when I got up, said goodnight to Karin and went to my room, thinking what the bellowing meant, why the mother wouldn't stay quiet.

And for the first time in my life, Mother, Louisiana is only a flat green place on the map, five thousand miles from here; when the cold comes it's an event, something Father still fears, worries over as he swaddles his azaleas in black plastic. The February I'm thinking about started out balmy, but mid-month an ice storm broke the redbud tree in the back-yard, ripped the limbs off so the tree looked as if someone took a bite of it, though the gash healed, gray now as the rest of the bark. I remember that morning you buttoned your blue coat in the foyer and pulled on black leather gloves I'd never seen.

"But I've had these for years," you said, shaking the second glove to make it flap like a blackbird. "Longer than I've had you."

I knew then they were some remnant of your life in Ohio, your childhood place, where my small, crinkled Grandma Minna lived in a white farmhouse I had seen once, the Christmas when the fields were buried under snow.

And as always when I thought of Grandma Minna I had an immediate, corresponding, contradictory image of Grandma Baye, large-boned and red-haired, barreling down the tiled hallway of the hospital in her black shoes, tapping a pencil against some child's chart and hollering for a nurse. The two women have been for me always two halves of a companion set—one as remote as the other was vivid and daily and bullying. They're both dead now. Minna died in her sleep one summer while I was at camp, but it was last week that Grandma Baye's funeral filled the First Baptist Church, where the black-robed choir sang "Will the Circle Be Unbroken" and Father wept beside me. Thirty-six hours later I was on a plane headed back to the ice, the whales, and why, for the first time in twenty years, to you, Mother?

I remember you flapped the black glove under my nose once more, then bent down and drew it on so I could see how it fastened with three small leather buttons. Your wrist at the leather cuff was thin and blue-veined.

We stood there, bundled, waiting for Baye Ellen. Even at eight years old she was slow, painstaking over her dress, combing and combing her long hair and then fussing with the clips, bands, bows. Your cheeks were pink and your dark blue irises brimmed with moisture. You held my mittened hand and smiled down at me, chattering about my first grade teacher and singing the "V-a-l-e-n-t-i-n-e" song from the day before, though even then I was slightly depressed by singing for a

163

leftover occasion. When Baye Ellen finally came down you helped her with her coat with more patience than you usually showed, and then you herded us onto the walk slick with frost. I walked in the grass to hear the thin ice crunch on each flattened blade, and Baye Ellen sang that she hoped my feet would be as wet and cold as they deserved to be.

Mother, what were you thinking as you stood, wrapped and silent on the concrete path to Pine Street School, waving goodbye to us, knowing we would never see you again? At the doorway I turned and ran back to you, nose running, blue knit cap pulled down to my eyebrows, ran back for the goodbye kiss that was ritual between us; Baye Ellen had already disappeared through the heavy oak doors of the school.

I reached up for your dark hair, the warm blue wool of your coat, your fragrance of spice and wilderness as you bent to take my kiss on your cold cheek.

"Be a good boy, John," you whispered.

That afternoon it was Father who waited for us outside the playground fence—Father with his taut face, brown eyes welling up as he watched us come forward. Baye Ellen ran right to him, but I stopped by the swings and wouldn't approach, wouldn't touch him. In the folds of his coat he carried the air of mischance, of your absence, and I began to scream for you, gripped the metal post of the swing set and couldn't be moved.

For a week we lived with Grandma Baye, but when we went back to our house I stood in Father's bedroom. The glass top of the dresser was bare, except for Father's square black hairbrush, and the tan silk drapes and quilted bedspread were new and masculine; Grandma Baye had hung the drapes herself, Geneva told me, the morning after your funeral. But the empty closet still faintly held your scent and the smell lingered all through the long spring afternoons I lay on the closet floor and waited for Father to come home. With the door closed, I sucked my thumb and listened to Geneva below me as she banged the pots in the kitchen and sang country songs she wrote herself.

Geneva had found you when she came to work at noon—wiry, black-haired Geneva Wright, who talked to me last week during a break at the LeCajun Club, where she still plays guitar though she is nearly eighty, and blind—and Geneva who told me how she'd heard the car idling in the garage. You were behind the wheel, still wearing your blue coat and gloves.

"She was just as pretty as you please," said Geneva, "like she was going calling and just misplaced in her mind where she ought to go."

Up here it's easy enough to make fast attachments—friendships of a few days take on the permanence of myth and last a lifetime; meet a man once and you never forget his name, or his face, or what season you were enduring when you met, or what he said.

Last night when I opened my door to her knock, Karin said, "Hey Johnny Boy, it's cold outside." She put her hands on my face and my cheeks stung. "Warm me," she said, and sat down on my bunk. She kicked off her boots and pulled her legs under her. "Here," she said, fishing a flask from her pocket. "Pour."

I handed her the glass with the brandy and she sniffed it, took a mouthful and settled on the bunk. I sat in my hard desk chair an arm's length away, the other side of the narrow room.

"Those stupid guys," she said. "I'd like to tell Vin and all the rest of them off."

"You'd better not," I warned her.

"They must be telling these stories for my benefit," she said. "To toughen me up."

"What else do they have to talk about? If you ask me, those whales are goners."

"Maybe," she said, flicking her hair back over her shoulder. Six of us work here on the Point, but Karen is the only woman, and the other biologists joke that she looks a little like a whale herself, with her small, wide-set gray eyes and puffy blond bangs low over her forehead. She's big and

165

sturdy-looking, attractive, but up here, one sees so few women. Karin's outsize frame seems slightly illusory, as if she's drawn to another scale, put into this picture by mistake.

"Was that true?" she said. "About that kid nursing?"

I nodded. "Remember those stories you read in school? Lost colonists who starved when winter set in? That rarely happened here."

"They're resourceful," she argued.

"They eat their dogs. Then their clothes. Then they cannibalize," I had to tell her. "Up in Kaktovik there's a woman who ate her husband and children one winter when their food ran out."

"Recently?" she said, frowning.

Karin is thirty or more, a few years older than I am. Still, she hasn't been up here long.

"No," I said. "A long time ago. Before our time. She's an old woman now." I took a drink of her brandy. "Relax," I told her. "They're Americans now. Nothing to worry about."

Mother, after your death Father took us to Grandma Baye's, the dark-papered, cypress-floored, high-ceilinged house of his birth. For thirty years, Grandma had her practice in one room on the first floor, but the whole house is Father's law office now, hemmed in on one side by a fried chicken restaurant and on the other by a long-distance telephone service. You wouldn't know the street today, Mother—nobody lives in the fine old houses anymore. Surely you heard the story that Grandma never wept when her husband enlisted during World War II and left her to run their practice alone, and raise Father. It's local legend: she went to the hospital the morning after the news of Grandfather's death came from Normandy and removed Carl Fontenot's tonsils just as she'd scheduled.

Sometimes it seems inconceivable that out of this tough old woman would come my tall, stooping, baffled father. But perhaps the Hollis Baye Chamblee he started out to be, twenty-five and a senior in law school at LSU the night you came to his fraternity party, was different from the man he's become. After Grandma Baye's funeral he spoke of you for the first time in years, keeping me up late until I believed I could almost see you, dark and bored, listening to the sibilant patter of Southern men and their girls in the heat of a Baton Rouge autumn hotter than any summer you must have spent in Ohio, walking out to the porch where Father argued politics with two of the brothers. He told me how, three days later, you kissed him hard on the mouth as you sat in the lounge watching election returns on TV; he told how, the next June, with Baye Ellen already tumbling in your womb, the two of you married and returned to live in Beauville. And he said you waited for his mother's wrath but it never came, that she was never more or less than polite to you from the first interminable dinner at her house until the end, when she kissed your cheek at Hinson's Funeral Home.

I could tell you now that it would have been better if you'd kept walking across the fraternity house porch that first night; if you'd tossed your drink into the shrubbery and walked alone back to Evangeline Hall, so after bed check and lights out you could lie awake thinking that you had had enough of the Spanish moss and mint julep crowd and your dotty Baton Rouge aunt who wanted you to see for yourself that the South wasn't as bad as the papers made it out to be. I can make you toss, sleepless, in the heat, make your fingers cramp as you fill out transfer applications to Kenyon, Wooster, Ohio State, even allow you to meet some square-jawed finance major from Columbus who would overcome your life with his prudent money and rash cheerfulness, allow you to buy trousseaus and linens and then baby blankets and bicycles and golf clubs and cocktails and your life would be one long unstoppable expense account whose balance never comes due. But that night standing on the porch of the Kappa Alpha house Hollis Chamblee was fueled by a lethal mix of bourbon and politics and you mistook it for passion, were sucked into it like a flame into a cigarette. Father, in his own cancerous lurch toward death, says that you were luminous, a dark-haired girl in a white sweater and full skirt, a ghostly figure in the shadows of the white columns of the fraternal order, so that when he turned to you and said, "Maybe you can tell these fools why Jack Kennedy's going to win," he was half expecting you not to speak, to be simply a trick of the light. But then you smiled, and came to stand beside him. "Why will he win?" you said. "Because you're going to vote for him."

I grew up knowing that I was born thirty minutes after President Kennedy died in a Dallas hospital, but didn't know that you sat in your hospital bed nursing me as you watched his funeral on television. Father says it chilled him to see your stricken face as you cradled me against you, my coming-home day already turned into a day of mourning. Baye Ellen claims to remember nothing of this time, sheltered as she was in the dark rooms of Grandma Baye's house while you held me in your white room in the Baptist Hospital. Far from your own birthplace, twenty-one, a mother of two with six years left to live—it was your unthinkable act of entering John Kennedy Chamblee on my birth certificate instead of John Baye, the name negotiated (Mary Baye for a girl) over dinner-table discussions with Father and my grandmother, that Grandma Baye couldn't forgive you for.

I've heard stories up here of women who've lived through the unendurable, who have watched their children freeze, who have seen babies eaten by wolves, who have walked to find food until their feet bled, who have hung their own children rather than have them suffer death by starvation.

When I was small I believed you had moved away, like the Wannermanns, who went to Texas. Grandma Baye, with a curious down-drooping of her mouth that even I noticed, said you went to live with Jesus, and perhaps this made me hold more tightly to my notion of your departure that first summer I grieved at her house, between innumerable lessons—swimming, baseball, gymnastics—you had never enlisted me in. The portrait of Jesus in the upstairs hallway showed a brooding man with shoulder-length hair and mild brown eyes, the hem of his flowing white robe puddled around his sandals, one hand raised to knock at a door. I knew it was your door he had touched, and when you answered his knock the two of you walked out into something I had seen on TV: a field where smiling, clapping people who wore beads and flowers held up their fingers in a vee when the camera panned over them. I heard the voices chanting for peace; I saw the mild-eyed Jesus sitting beside a dark-haired woman, and glimpsed her face as she bent to diaper their fat, leg-kicking baby. And I knew by the curve of the woman's neck that she was you, that this was the life you had made for yourself away from us.

Perhaps it was then that I contrived to hate you. The woman in the blue coat smelling of cold became a woman whose face contorted with rage, whose fingers pinched into my shoulders, who screamed "Who said you could touch that?" as shards of the broken vase dug into my fingers. I began to stockpile your worst moments as a mother—all of your quick, dangerous rages spilled out before me as if from an overturned bottle, and I knew again your fingernails cutting crescents into my arms; your shove backward that cracked my head against the doorknob; your stinging fingers on my cheek as the smart word left my lips.

Baye Ellen has willed away all of this. Within a few days of your death Sheila Shirley's mother took her under wing, filled her with cookies and tales of plucky motherless girls. When I stood beside her in church I noticed Baye Ellen even smelled like the Shirley's house, a whiff of lemon wax and butter mints. Her braids were more smoothly braided, her socks more neatly cuffed than ever before.

When I asked her last week what she remembered about you Baye Ellen's first response was a blank look, then she shook her head. "I was just a little girl," she said, rocking her youngest child by the fire. "What do you expect me to remember?"

In my narrow room, Karin talked about growing up without ever seeing snow. She took off her gray and white Icelandic sweater, then leaned back again on the bed in her white turtleneck and jeans, red sock feet pressed together sole to sole in a guru's pose. The glass of brandy sat untouched in the corral her bent knees made as she talked about ocean temperatures and annual migrations. She talked about her tiny wood-shingled house in San Diego and her work at the Scripps Institute. As the night wore on she talked about the lovers she had in college, her three abortions, her ex-husband and their child who died at only a few months old. She talked about discovering the emptiness that lies at the heart of any kind of love, the revelation that love is a chemical stimulus produced by the contact of one endocrine system with another. She talked about the foolhardy whales who forgot to go home and their feeble chances of survival. She said they're stupid, this mother and calf, for not staying with their own kind, for venturing after food or maybe just following a sound into the bay where the ice froze them in. She talked of need, of hunger; the eight-thousand-mile migration the whales make just to find food and a place to mate; she shook her head and told me of the captive whale at Scripps who carried her dead calf in her mouth for hours; divers finally harpooned the calf at the surface when the mother came up for air, and when the calf was gone the mother called and called, a sonorous low bellowing. But we're both scientists; we both knew without saying it that the severest distress call for a whale is silence, a slow voiceless sinking.

Father is thinner than I've ever seen him, large-framed but gaunt with the cancer that's already eaten part of his lungs. We worked in the yard side-by-side my last day at home, not hurrying, not even sweating in the mild afternoon sunlight. Leaves of oak, dogwood and redbud scattered and whirled around us.

"Now your mother," he said, "was one for leaves. When we moved in, it was her idea to cut the pines around the house and replant with deciduous. Everyone else still has their pines." He gestured with his rake handle to the neighbors' houses, and I thought he looked wistful, but whether for their

170

clean lawns or for you I don't know. He shook his head and went back to raking.

Barbara came out to the front porch and stood with her hands on her hips. She's slim, blond, a hard-muscled athletic woman who plays a lot of golf.

"Hollis," she called after she'd watched us a few minutes. "Lunch is ready. You too, John."

As we walked to the house together I felt as if I was borrowing someone else's life, as if the picture of father and son entering the house of a good woman who will replenish them with good food included me by mistake. Father married Barbara when I was in college and I feel like company when I visit them, though for all Barbara's remodeling and redecorating of your house, she didn't touch my room, still a dingy nest at the end of their white-walled, peach-carpeted hallway.

Father sat down on the brick step to take off his shoes and I stood over him, slipped off my sneakers. His hair is still dark except for tufts of white at the temples, and despite the thinness his face is good-looking and craggy. I have trouble thinking of him as a man who's dying. For a dozen years after your death he didn't bring other women home, wanting perhaps to spare Baye Ellen and me the pain of another attachment. But that day in the yard I realized I no longer considered him your husband: he was only a tall man in khakis and a green sweater, smelling of earth, smelling of leaves, slipping his feet into houseshoes left for him at the door. After lunch he worked on a few briefs, watched football on TV, dozed before dinner. A family man; Barbara told me that in Grandma's last long illness, he read to her every night from dog-eared copies of *The New England Journal of Medicine* while she swore and fretted disbelief at any new finding.

He turned his lined face toward me. "In winter I can stand upstairs in my bedroom," he said, "and see our whole house reflected in the neighbors' living room window, no shelter at all." He stands, hand on the doorknob. "Now why would she want to do that, do you think?"

Outside somewhere ice knocked against ice and the chainsaws revved. I wondered what the whales were doing in that darkness, in water so cold that if one of us fell in he'd be dead in under three minutes. Earlier Karin and I had stood alongside the channel and seen the two whales surfacing, lifting their vast, blotched heads, swimming close alongside each other and occasionally we heard their strange, muffled cries, low, deep-throbbing vibrations that seemed to shake the ice beneath us.

Standing there, Karin had turned to me, slipped her gloved hand around my arm and said, "A whale can sing for half an hour, and then repeat the same song, tone for tone."

The mother whale surfaced and blew, and then called out again.

"What's she telling him?" I said.

But before Karin could answer the calf called back, clear and penetrating.

"You tell *me*," Karin said.

I looked at the mother's gray snout crusted with barnacles and smelled the stench of the spray she blew. " 'It's every man for himself now, kiddo,' " I said.

Karin didn't smile. "When do you think it's ever been anything else?" she said, and squeezed my arm.

In my room, in the light of my desk lamp, Karin reached out for me and her hand collided with my chest; she slipped it up and over my shoulder and pulled me back with her onto the bed. "I just need somebody to hold me," she whispered. She put her mouth over my mouth and then pulled back. "Listen," she said. "They're doing it again. Tone for tone."

In my father's house Barbara's needlework shows up in little flourishing statements on pillows, wall hangings, a crewel rug. The dim garage is a family room. Where the automatic door used to be, a big bay window looks over the front yard. A stone fireplace, panelled walls and thick carpeting make it cozy. The afternoon after Grandma Baye's funeral, Baye Ellen came to the house with her three children and gynecologist husband and they tumbled over each other on the floor, on the immense soft sea of honey brown pile. From her days as a fraternity housemother, Barbara can make a snack for any occasion: that afternoon we had oatmeal cookies and hot buttered rum. I sat on plump, pumpkin-colored cushions in the window bay and watched the leaves fall across the yard. I was leaving the next morning for Alaska, coming back to work, back to winter darkness and forty-five below. But in what felt to me like warm weather Barbara wore a sweater against the chill and Father rose from his chair to put another log on the fire. He and the gynecologist talked amiable politics; Father votes Republican now, is even campaigning for a hot-shot state senator not much older than I am.

I was tired of talking with the women. Chief among Baye Ellen's whispered confidences that day was her husband's plan to open a Pit Grill franchise after Christmas. Mother, her face is so bland, a pink, smiling circle; she looks like no one in particular, but she has your straight brown hair. She cuts hers, though, blunt across the back of her neck. She has turned out so capable and perky, the plucky Anne of Green Gables, Nancy Drew, Cherry Ames, that I'll bet none of her friends believe or remember she's a suicide's daughter.

Barbara passed me a plate of cookies, and smiled at me from the sofa. The new log lit, Father backed into his chair, gray-faced suddenly. Baye Ellen's husband took advantage of the break to blow a raspberry on his son's stomach. Father looked uncertainly around the room until he focused on me. "You there, John," he called. His voice was thin and high. He motioned me to join the men, where I knew I'd be called on to argue, to defend my name, my politics, my preference for an icy climate. I turned instead to the window, where October darkness was settling down. Migrant birds huddled on the bare branches of your trees.

Last night I sat silent as a totem, smelling Karin's faint warm sourness and holding her as she turned out the light and then leaned against me on the bed. Punishment for wickedness and vice, lust, loathing, the eternal chatterings of ill feeling stored in our simple hearts: this was the story Karin poured out to me last night in my Spartan room, her breath warm on my neck and her fingers on my chest. Maybe she wanted the dark so I couldn't see her blotched face and dripping nose, but I heard the tears in her voice and the current of her ragged grief rising.

In Karin's story I learned about a small, shingled house where a child was put to bed for the night. When his mother, breasts aching, woke and realized he'd missed his feeding, she felt the enormous relief born out of months of broken nights; she believed his failure to wake was a sign of maturation, acclimatization to the world she'd delivered him to.

Her hard breasts were heavy and huge and she couldn't go back to sleep no matter how she tossed beside her husband, no matter how many messages she sent to her breasts telling them not to make milk in the middle of the night. In the bathroom she unbuttoned her nightgown and with the heels of her palms she brought down milk until it splattered the sink. She felt enormous, animal, a cow spurting into a pail.

Her son was a light sleeper so she tiptoed into his room and by the hallway light looked at his face webbed with the deep sleep of the newborn. She touched him gently, then began to shake him, finally slapping him on the back in an attempt to rouse him from her own worst nightmare. When she lifted him from his crib his face and hands were still faintly warm.

She held me against her as she cried for her lost child. I sat without speaking, listening to her tell me that she didn't want to live after her son died, that she had to come up here to get away from the loss, and from her husband, bitter now and blaming her, convinced their son's death was her punishment. "All of us up here are running from something," she said. "You don't have to be here long to see that." Finally, to quiet her I told the Inuit story of a child whose tribe was forced into cannibalism one fierce winter when hunting was poor. The Inuit say the child walked over the sea to another land where she became a princess; in this incarnation she forgave them everything, and with her forgiveness they no longer needed to feel remorse.

Mother, as I lay there holding a woman still strange to me, I was once again in the room where the dark green shades are drawn against the light. You sent me to my room to think so I lie on my high wooden sleigh bed and think about your hand gripping my shirt, lifting me through the air easily as Baye Ellen lifts her dolls. You are not weak, as Grandma Baye thinks. Your arms are finely muscled and your hands strong. I lie on the bed thinking of all the ways I've made you unhappy in the hour or so that I've been home from school. You have put my construction paper heart full of valentines on a high shelf. The satin box of Whitman's chocolates with the cherry cordials missing has been put in the freezer. Bits of the forbidden chocolate are wedged in my molars. The red print of your hand glows on my cheek.

I hear you walking up the stairs and I lie still, pretending to sleep. The door lets in light from the hall, then closes again, and you cross the room. You lie down beside me, Mother, you who screamed so recently for me to get out of your sight, that you could no longer bear to look at such a child. But you have often come here after your rage passes so I turn to you without ceremony and bury my head in your thin chest. Your strong arms hold me. You smell sweet and bitter like the sharp smell of snapped twigs. Weeping, you promise you will never hurt me again, never strike me. As you whisper I let your strong fingers smooth my hair, let your hands press me against you until I feel we must be one body, one frightened, trembling creature hiding from your demons. And you are still murmuring to me when you fall asleep and I lie awake beside you watching the light bleed away from the windows.

Guided by instinct, by the salt stirrings of their own warm blood, the whales made a stupid mistake. They made their way from the warm waters of Baja, California through the Bering Strait, into the waiting arms of an ice shelf that would not let them go. When the rest of their herd made the long, lazy turnaround in the freezing waters and headed south, the mother and calf stayed behind. For food; out of curiosity; because they have no sense of direction—everyone has a theory. But because whales are big, gentle, intelligent beings we watched them with a mixture of bemusement and horror. Because we are scientists, we want to know why the instinct fails, why creatures are no longer interested in protecting themselves. So for over a week we cut away the ice and measure temperatures, time the intervals between their surfacings. The President telephones. Reporters arrive. A *National Geographic* crew shoots a cover story. We drink coffee and wait for the icebreaker that will free them; we wait for the whales to stop breathing. The Inuit on the shoreline do not want the whales to die, but in the long wait they can sometimes be heard making hypothetical plans for the blubber, the meat, the baleful eyes that gleam on the periphery of the animals' monstrous foreheads. And this morning, Mother, just hours before the icebreaker arrived all of us were called from our beds because the calf had stopped surfacing. The mother didn't dive for the body but she wouldn't leave either, even when the icebreaker chiseled out a path for her to follow. And her cry was almost human in its timbre of grief. "Get out of here, you stupid bitch," Vin shouted at the whale, waving his fists, and Karin slapped him hard. We watched the mother bleakly. Her great bulk filled the narrow channel; she could barely turn around. *Lumaa, lumaa* resonated off the ice but as I stood there listening I understood finally that this was less an accusation than an indelible statement of circumstance. When at last the whale swam behind the icebreaker into the open sea we found we didn't have the heart to monitor her further.

Mother, as the whale moved steadily away from us through the polar darkness, I wished it were me she trailed dumbly in her wake. Karin cheered along with everybody else; she cried, she caught up my hand and pressed it to her freezing lips. But when I bent to hear what she was saying, her voice in my ear was the wind over an enormous distance.

About the Author

Charlotte Holmes was educated at Louisiana State University and Columbia University, and was a Wallace Stegner Fellow at Stanford University. Her stories have appeared in *The Antioch Review, Epoch, Grand Street, The New Yorker, STORY,* and other magazines. In 1993 she won the Writers Exchange award sponsored by Poets and Writers, Inc., and has received fellowships from the Pennsylvania Arts Council and the Bread Loaf Writers' Conference. She is an associate professor of English at the Pennsylvania State University, and lives in State College, Pennsylvania with her husband and son.